The Dybbuk

ANGELA DARLING

DEDICATION

For Jeannie. Who helped open my eyes to both the good and the bad.
I am forever in your debt.

For Jaime. Who, without that terrifying night with the Ouija board,
this book would not exist.

PROFOUND THANKS

Abha Kalra
Alexander Lo
Amy Brooks
Andrew Dickinson
Ashley Gonzalez
Becky Rusnak
Brandon Jones
Bruce Waldron
Cathy McVay
Cheryl Martin
Craig Dockstader
Danyal Spadoni
David Tovar
Eric Calvin
Faith Ulate
Heather Goodin
Helene Bouffard
Jackson Deerfield
Jean Lanctot
Jesica Lancaster
Jim Lamond
Jon Quiett
Juanita Clark
Karen Pritchett
Katie Baxter
Keri Brinton
Lani Bartelt
Lisa Betancourt
Lois Leick
Maia Place
Margaret Denton
Martina Dalton
Mary Shuford
Meaghan McClure
Michael Peterson
Michelle Balatico
Mike Raglin
Miranda Cheyenne
Monica Lorance
Nate Milatz
Nazar Gamdysey
Nicolas Mora
Omar Barroso

Ahmed Ali
Ali Cobb
Andi Benoit
Angie Triplett
Autumn Short
Berik Bassline
Brian Schell
Bryan Burgmaier
Chantal Bumgarner
Chuck Cockrum
Dacre Stoker
Daryl Marincovich
Donny McCleery
Eric Lin
Glenn Stenson
Heather Patackas
Ian Ludwig
Jaime Loveless
Jeannie Martin-Sago
Jessy Fosness
Jimmy Fox
Josh Anon
Juanita Williams
Karna Thorsby
Kazuki Kitamura
Kim Snyder
Laura Sechier
Lisa Call
Loni Gordon
Maile Cabral
Mariam Anderson
Mark Galanti
Matlock Highbarger
Melissa Curnel-Pendleton
Michael Taylor
Michelle Sofie
Mike Sechrist
Mischka Leonti
Nanette Nanjo-Jones
Nathalie Becker
Nicholas Marcel
Njoku Peter
Pam Bolter

Alain Sauvage
Allison Lynch
Andrea Jean
Anna-Marie Bannigan
Barbara Hawryszczak
Bert Rutherford
Brooke Brown
Caroline Dennewith
Charlene Ostrom
Courtney Nicholson
Danny Tong
David Renfroe
Emily Tillman
Erik Simonson
Heather Alderson
Helen Tawake
Izzy Parker
Janene Coltom
Jennifer Read
Jill Rubin Siegel
Joe Lawrence
JR Salmon
Karen Fosness
Kasey Watters
Kellye Paterson
Kristin Woods
Lionel Harvey
Lois Leavitt Marquart
Lynn Quiriarte
Margaret Bush
Marie Progl
Mary McLean
Matthew Silver
Michael Griswold
Michael Weiss
Michelle von Eschen
Mike Stanfield
Mohamed Slili
Natasha Allen
Nathan Troudt
Nick Lane
Olivia Worth
Pamela Curnel

Pasquale DeMaio
Portia Gregg
Rahul Swarnkar
Rannell Alsteen
Richard Weller
Robert Starcher
Ronnie Payton
Ryan Ocholik
Sani Liu
Scott Schwartz
Shane Hall
Shelby Fitzgerald
Stacie Stoney
Steven Reed
Tadd Armbruster
Taneika Sadewasser
Thuan Nguyen
Tina Tyler
Vickie Brown
Vladimir Lysikov

Paul Adamson
Rachel Brannberg
Ramon Sanchez
Rene Coelho
Rick Jackson
Rodney Brewer
Ryan Collins
Ryan Pang
Sarah Dunsmore
ShaChrista Winters
Shanna Turek
Shelia Foster
Stanton Brown
Stu Reed
Tamara Schemp
Tasha Jamison
Tim Kendrick
Tony Searles
Viliame Leger
Will Simajaya

PJ Ronnebaum
Ragni Singh
Randy DeBolt
Richard Burgin
Robert Beller
Ron Ross
Ryan Gohlinghorst
Sam Rivas
Sarah Robinson
Shane Castillo
Shari Sauceda
Spike Bowden
Steve Woods
Syouyou Suzuki
Tami Cornwell
Theador Coal
Tim Mahoney
Trevor Gunderson
Vince Soto
William Green

CONTENTS

ACKNOWLEDGMENTS

I'd like to thank the people of Peru for their kindness and warmth and for

sharing their rich culture and hospitality with me.

"Do not be afraid; our fate cannot be taken from us; it is a gift."

~ Dante Alighieri, Inferno

FOREWORD

It's been a difficult few years for me...

Something tragic happened that shook my faith to its core. And I buckled when I should have held firm. I started asking myself unanswerable questions; I became bitter. I pushed the idea of religion out of my life. I had no time for useless things.

I balked at anything spiritual because of that anger. I had once been a person that believed in a reason for everything, a purpose cloaked deep within any tragedy. But there was finally something terrible that had no reason.

There was nothing to be gained. Nothing to be learned. Only questions left lingering in the air, never to be answered.

I don't bring up this story to depress or air my own dirty spiritual laundry. I only mention it because it's important to know, when reading this story, where my mind was.

Despite all my unforgiving anger, I never once doubted the existence of the dark side of man. Something powerful beyond our reach and our understanding that only wishes to do us harm. And yet why was I so fervently willing to believe in the existence of evil and not of good?

It was because of that one night I stupidly played with a Ouija board.

A girlfriend and I were over at one of her friend's house. We were young, stupid, and drinking. Someone brought out a Ouija board. We messed around with it a little bit, laughing and carrying on. It was all a joke. Just some silly little thing to do while downing more alcohol.

And then at some point only me and my best friend were playing with it. It began to move. I looked up with alarm at my friend and she was giving me the same look. There are a handful of people that I trust implicitly with my life; that I would take a bullet for and know they would take a bullet for me. My best friend is one of them.

This was not her playing a cruel joke. Because she was just as terrified as I was.

Following is the conversation with this…thing as best as I can recall:

Me: Do you know anyone here?

It: Yes.

Me: Do you know me?

It: Yes.

Me: What year did you die?

It: 1778.

Me: What is your name?

It: (At this point it spelled out some oddly unpronounceable name; it sounded like a Slavik name)

Me: What do you want?

It: Hurt.

Me: Did I hurt you?

It: Yes.

Me: Did I break your heart? (I prodded, terrified of knowing where this conversation was heading and trying to not take it where I felt it was going).

It shot the planchette over to No, as if it was angered that I would have the gall to suggest such a notion.

Me: Did I kill you?

It: Yes.

I had heard enough. My friend and I took our hands off the board and have never touched one since.

I don't know what we were speaking with that night, but I knew enough that I should not have been playing with things I don't understand.

I felt foolish and silly that I may have opened the door a little bit to something that should not have been spoken with in the first place. Perhaps not a door was opened, but I certainly dusted off an old chest and peeked inside.

I didn't like what I saw.

My friend tried to comfort me, telling me that if it was true, that if I had killed someone in a past life, that I must have had a good reason for it.

But I knew this thing for what it was.

A liar.

It was trying to bait me into something. And I refused to bite.

Why, then, after coming face to face with something ominous did I so quickly dismiss the idea of something good? Something protective? Was it because it has never proven itself in so obvious a fashion to me before? That the good things leisurely arrived in my life, so modestly that I could never see them?

My grandmother had a stroke when I was a teenager; she was in the hospital and my family was planning on going up to see her. She had been in the hospital for some time and this trip was one of many. But I had a babysitting job that I had lined up for myself that day.

It may seem rather trivial a decision looking back on it now, how silly and obvious the choice was, but I actually was torn. I really needed the money and my grandmother had been in the hospital for some time now. Surely, I could go tomorrow.

I asked for a sign; some help to figure out what to do.

Often when people ask for signs, they rarely get them. And I honestly wasn't expecting anything.

But then the phone rang.

It was the woman who had hired me for the babysitting job; she found someone else. I was free.

I went to visit my grandmother.

She died that night.

Again, I don't bring up these stories as a means of trying to be persuasive about religion, beliefs, or anything of that nature. If you ask any of my friends, you'll find that I'm the last person who will debate religion or politics. Frankly, there's plenty of other stuff I'd rather be doing.

But I bring this up to set up the tale you're about to read.

Bree is a lot like where I'm at right now. Not a devout anything, really. She grew up with religion but as she got older, she began to question things herself and trying to find out where it fit in her life.

So, when these things begin to happen to her, it shakes her into believing. She believes in the good because of the evil. It's a roundabout and terrible route to lead to religious faith, but a sadly effective one.

It's a balance of the universe; good cannot exist without evil just as evil cannot exist without good.

I guess what it comes down to is your choice: in your life, which one are you going to let win?

~ Angela Darling

Ephraim Moses Lilien, 1908{{PD-US}}

CHAPTER ONE
THE NINTH STONE

April 2000

"911, what is your emergency?"

"….my dad… he's lying on the floor. Please come, he's lying on the floor bleeding…"

"Okay, sweetheart, what's your address?"

"Um…it's… it's 9561 Evergreen Road."

"Alright, hon, we've got units dispatched and on their way. What's your name?"

"My name…" Sob. "My name is Bree."

"Okay, Bree. What happened to your dad?"

"I don't know…"

"How old are you, Bree?"

"I'm eight."

"Okay, Bree. I want you to tell me what happened."

"I just woke up and came downstairs because my Mom was calling my name…and my Dad was lying here. I don't think he's breathing."

"Where is your mother? Can I speak with her?"

"Um… ma'am… she can't talk right now."

"What do you mean, Bree?"

Sob.

"Bree, Bree, are you there? Don't hang up on me, okay? I want you to stay with me until the units get there, okay?"

Sniffle. "Okay."

"Bree, why can't you put your Mom on the phone?"

"She... she won't talk right."

"...what do you mean 'she won't talk right?'"

"...she's just talking funny, ma'am. She's not making any sense. Listen."

.... "I was right, I was right... it's the ninth stone, the ninth stone all along...and I told him but he didn't.... he didn't... he didn't listen... Oh goddamn you... Goddamn you back to whereever you came from!!!!"

Shuffle.

"Bree?"

"Yes, ma'am."

"Did she say the 'ninth stone?'"

"I think so."

"What does that mean?"

"I don't know. She just keeps repeating it. She's sitting in the corner on the floor just saying it over and over."

Sob.

"Ma'am, her eyes don't look right. Her eyes...just don't look right."

Sirens.

"Bree, I think the units are almost there, okay, hon? I can hear them."

Sob.

"Bree?"

Soft crying.

"Bree?"

"….yes, ma'am?"

"You are a very brave little girl. You did the right thing by calling me, okay?"

"Okay."

"Okay, I'm going to hang up now, Bree, as the officers are almost there."

"Wait…. Ma'am?"

"Yes, Bree?"

"…. will the policeman take him away?"

"Take who away, Bree?"

…………..

"Bree?"

…………..

"Bree, are you there?"

Sirens approaching.

"Bree!"

"…ma'am… he's coming down the stairs… he's looking right at me…"

"Bree, who is? Is there someone in the house with you?"

"Yes."

"Who is it?"

"I don't know. But he doesn't look right."

"What do you mean he doesn't look right?"

"His… his eyes. His eyes are black…"

June 2019

She jolted awake, a small cry escaping her lips. She could immediately taste salt; her body was covered in sweat. As usual, her heart thudded rapidly in her chest, hammering so hard she had to lie back and try to meditate on other things before it would slow down again.

But this time it wouldn't work.

"Fuck."

She threw her feet over the side of her bed and sat in the dark for a moment, holding her head in her hands.

Far off in the distance she heard the sound of an ambulance, a car alarm going off incessantly, someone down on the street yelling at another person.

Ah, New York.

She got up and padded onto the chipped tile of her bathroom, opened the medicine cabinet. Perused several different prescription bottles.

Prozac, Celexa, Paxil, Norpramin, Pamelor… the list went on and on. She reached for the Prozac and knocked a bottle of Metamucil into her toilet bowl. Bree just smiled and thought it a fitting place. She turned the faucet on and got herself a glass of water.

She opened the bottle and popped a few pills into her palm, swigging a long drag of water with it. For a moment she stood there in the dark bathroom, staring at her reflection, the only light coming in through the slightly parted curtains of her bedroom behind her.

The fluorescent "Closed" sign from the sushi restaurant on the first story of her building was always obnoxiously casting a red glow over her furniture. It made her apartment look semi-ominous once she turned the lights out at night. But it was a rent-controlled apartment in SoHo. She had a winning lottery ticket. She wasn't going to nitpick.

Bree glanced up hesitantly to the dirty mirror. Her face looked tired, drawn.

Old.

An old woman. War waged lines prematurely on her face. Old at 27.

19 years. She sighed heavily, her shoulders drooping sloppily in her nightshirt. 19 years later and it still haunted her...

An odd buzzing sound came from the bedroom and she smiled. She turned the corner into her room and saw the faint blue glow from her cell phone on the nightstand.

How did he always know?

"R U up?"

Bree smiled and typed: "Yes."

"U had it again?"

Her smiled broadened and she shook her head, lying back onto the bed and typing out, "Yes."

"Fuck, B. Call me if u need to."

Her smile settled and she put the phone aside and crawled back under the covers. For a while she lay in the dark, staring up at the ceiling, the red glow from the sign outside draping a crimson curtain over the tops of her furniture. The small ticking of the old bell alarm clock on her nightstand was reassuring. She refused to get one of the new digital clocks; she was a curmudgeon to change.

Plus, this clock had been her Grandmother's…

…her eyes drooped, the previous nightmare all but forgotten.

Bree was awake and cooking some eggs when she heard the knock on the door. David was there, holding out a disposable paper cup from The Bean, their favorite coffee shop.

"Latte?"

"Mmm… Good morning to you too," she grabbed the cup and took a long sip. "Have you eaten?"

"Nah, I just rushed over here from my place. Haven't had a chance," David said, sitting down at the small dining table, taking off his knit hat. His hair was unruly and badly in need of a trim.

Bree laughed at him as she broke another egg into the pan. "You couldn't even bring yourself to brush your hair for me?"

He smiled, a light dimple dancing on the corner of his mouth and then it was gone. "Nah. Not worth the effort. I knew the coffee would win you over."

"Bare minimum kind of guy, eh?" She smiled, setting down a plate of eggs in front of him.

He rolled up his sleeves, grabbed a fork and began shoveling the food into his mouth. "I like to keep my expectations low. People never expect much out of me. Then I can be a hero when I do something as simple as brushing my hair. Or flirting with Rachel down at The Bean to get a free latte."

"Charming," she replied, wiping her hands on a towel and grabbing her plate. She sat down across from him and ate silently. David was done with his food before her and he sipped his coffee, staring at her patiently.

Exasperated, she finally put her fork down and looked him in the eye.

"Yes, I had that damn dream again, okay?"

"That makes, what, five times this month?"

"So far, yes."

"A bit excessive, don't you think?"

Bree picked up her fork and poked mindlessly at her eggs. She nodded.

He drew a deep breath. She knew what he was going to say; she let him say it anyway.

"Think you should go back and see Dr. Thiele?"

"Waste of time," she replied bitterly. "All he's going to say is to exercise more, get more rest, meditate, take another pill... useless." She shook her head. "Fucking useless."

"Well, does it help just to talk about it? You know, since you won't talk about it with me?"

Bree looked up, her gaze meeting his. She softened.

"Davey, it's not that I don't trust you. It's just family bullshit that I don't want to burden you with. And I..." She looked down again, not wanting to continue the conversation.

David prodded.

"And you what?"

"I… I just don't want you to think any less of me. You know, because of my family."

"No, actually. I don't know."

She glanced up, frustrated.

"All I *do* know is that whatever this dream is it terrifies the hell out of you," he continued. "And I worry about you. Of course, I do. We've been friends for a long time; I know when something's wrong."

"Davey… Davey, I'm fine."

"Are you?"

She met his gaze and managed a wan smile. "Yes. Everything's fine."

He rubbed the bridge of his nose and sighed deeply. He pulled his hat back on and leaned across the table to kiss her forehead.

"When you're ready, you'll tell me." His dark honey eyes were serious and concerned, not a hint of his usual sarcasm and humor. Then he stood.

"You'd better get your ass moving or you'll be late again. I'll talk to you later."

Bree watched him walk to the door. He hesitated for a moment, turned to her with that serious look in his eyes. Her stomach dropped a bit, anticipating the start of a difficult conversation with David that she didn't want to have.

"Oh, and B?" He asked.

"Yeah?"

The playful twinkle was back. He grinned. "Thanks for the eggs."

He winked and then he was gone.

She understood obsession. That gnawing feeling that if only you looked at something a different way, came at it from a different direction, then maybe the unsolvable could be answered.

The drone of office sounds buzzed around her; phones ringing, the copier spitting out paper after paper, the din of voices talking about depositions, trial dates, billable hours.

Through the thick of it all she had let her curiosity get the better of her, yet again, and did an internet search for "The Ninth Stone." And again, she was met with disappointment. Nothing tangible or relatable to the drivel that her mother spewed out that night.

The dreams are one thing, Breanna, she told herself silently, closing out her browser search window. *This is another. You have to let this go.*

"Hey, did you hear?" Someone came upon her suddenly and she jumped and turned. It was Veronica, an intern that had been with the company for a few months. In that time she and Breanna had a few lunches together and she had attached herself to Bree quite desperately. Bree felt a little bad for her and did everything she could to be kind.

"I'm sorry if I scared you, Bree. Did you hear about Carlisle? It's all over the news."

Her skin crawled but she did her best not to show it. Nobody knew. Nobody knew who she was. She intended to keep it that way.

Veronica grabbed her arm and pulled her over to the media room where a handful of attorneys and admins were huddled, watching the unfolding press conference.

Sheriff Marr was standing in front of a podium, his haggard face drawn into a look of permanent sternness.

"At 10am tomorrow, convicted murderer Randall Carlisle will be released from Sullivan Correctional facility. Mr. Carlisle was convicted in 2000 for the murder of Joseph Ward, a general contractor from Queens. He was given a life sentence but is being released early for good behavior. As city sheriff I've been sworn to uphold justice and to treat every individual fairly and equally under the law. Mr. Carlisle has been evaluated by the top mental health doctors in the state and has been found to be competent and, I believe, can become an active member of society.

"I will not be accepting any further questions at this time," Sheriff Marr began to walk away from the podium but was flooded with reporters shouting out questions eagerly to the officer, hoping to be heard.

A chill ran down Bree's spine and she looked down to the floor. She tried to ignore the high fives and hollers that the attorneys gave one another. Their voices blending together with, "I told you he wasn't guilty." "I knew he'd get paroled." "He's just too nice a guy to have done that."

Randall Carlisle was a very charismatic man. And educated too.

He had been a professor at a prestigious school teaching archaeology. He went to work every morning, came home to a wife and child every night, ate dinner with them, graded papers, went to sleep.

He also snuck into a house in the middle of the night twenty years ago and murdered a beloved father.

"Can you believe it, Bree? Paroled early. Never thought I'd see the day," Veronica gushed, shaking her head as she watched the attorneys continue to celebrate.

Softly, Bree replied, "Neither did I."

Two hours later saw her on a bus heading east towards Fallsburg. She had faked a migraine to get out of work and hopped on the earliest bus she could.

Before she left, she made a quick phone call to David about her plan and he voiced his concern.

"Are you sure that's wise, B? Going to see him? Why on earth would you want to do that?"

David knew about her father, Mr. Joseph Ward, being murdered at the hands of this man but he didn't know everything. Bree couldn't tell him everything. The only people in the world whose opinions mattered to her were her grandmother's and David's. She didn't want to sully that with concern that she was crazy.

"I have to, Davey. It's hard for me to explain. And I don't expect you to understand."

"You're right. I don't understand because I don't know the whole story. Yet again."

He sighed begrudgingly into the phone.

"But I trust you, Bree. Completely. And if this is something that you feel you need to do to get closure, you know I'm behind you. I just wish you would have told me earlier. I would have come with you."

"I know you would have, Davey. I didn't find out myself until just today," she replied.

"You mean no one called to tell you before the press conference that they were going to let this asshole out?"

"Well, I imagine they couldn't find me."

The line went quiet for a moment; David was trying to grapple with what she was telling him.

"I took my maternal surname after my father's death. Went to live with my Grandma Doris, my dad's mom. Moved out and disappeared when I was old enough. I imagine they were looking for a grown woman named Breanna Ward."

"I see," he said softly and then sighed. "Well, I'll be waiting for you when you get back into town."

Bree smiled in spite of herself and replied, "I know you will be. Thank you for understanding, Davey."

That conversation had gone over easier than she had planned. It was the conversation she was eventually going to have to have with her grandmother that she was dreading.

The bus jolted to a stop in the middle of a blocked road.

"Fallsburg!" The driver yelled and opened the door. Bree grabbed her purse and alighted from the bus. The main street of the town was surprisingly packed. News vans and reporters bustled around the sidewalk, likely camping out until the morning. Every station wanted to be the first to film the notorious Randall Carlisle walking out of the prison gates a free man.

Bree saw a Café sign and ran to the door, the crowd of reporters milling around her obnoxiously, unaware of who this woman was in relation to the hot story of the moment. The café inside was small and dimly lit but completely packed. Every seat in the place was filled with an eager reporter sipping on coffee or chowing down on a late lunch.

Her head spun and she found it hard to catch her breath. The heat in the cramped café didn't help; she found a ladies' restroom which was, blessedly, unoccupied and turned the water on. Splashed some cold water on her face.

Studied at herself in the dinghy mirror. It wasn't until she was standing there, gripping the side of the cold sink, that she began to doubt herself.

What am I doing here? This is lunacy. The man will not be able to give me any information I don't already know. I should just hop on the bus and go back home to my comfortable apartment, leave the past behind me. Shy away from any news reports on the television, because I know there will be plenty. Eventually the interest will die away and I can go back to my life of relative obscurity.

But she understood obsession.

That gnawing feeling that if only you looked at something a different way, came at it from a different direction, then maybe the unsolvable could be answered.

This was her last chance. Before he disappeared into a throng of people and she missed her opportunity. To ask him the question that she had so longed to have answered since it happened.

And every year, every month, every day since then.

Why?

Resolved, she wiped her hands on a paper towel and then went to the busy counter of the restaurant.

A haggard older gentleman saw her and made his way over. "What can I get for you, Miss?"

"Just some information, if you have it."

He smiled lightly, looking relieved that he didn't have yet another demanding customer on his hands. "Of course."

"How do I get to the prison from here?"

He shook his head briefly but then began giving her directions. The buildings were on a sharp upslope over the Neversink River. No cars were allowed up the road per prison orders. She would have to hoof it.

She smiled and thanked him for his help, slipping a $10 bill across the counter.

Then she was gone.

The guard in the cramped office asked for her name; when she gave it, he disappeared for a few minutes. Came back with a stern look on his face.

"I'm sorry, Ms. Adams, but Mr. Carlisle is not having visitors at this time."

Her heart sank a bit. She never imagined that she would come all this way and he could just refuse to see her.

"Perhaps you can tell him that Breanna Ward is here."

"Ward?" He asked, his eyebrows raising suspiciously.

She nodded. "Yes, just tell him Breanna Ward is here to see him."

He disappeared again.

She sat waiting in the stuffy, small office, looking up at police stories featuring apprehended criminals and wanted posters of dangerous looking men. The hands on the clock told her it was almost 2pm. The day was almost gone. And she still didn't have any of the answers she wanted.

The guard finally returned, his face looking a little less stern. Though slightly confused.

"Mr. Carlisle will see you. Have a seat and I'll let you know when he's ready."

She sat down, an odd rush of relief and apprehension gripping her. Bree was excited but also terrified to see Randall face to face. The last time she had seen him…

"Miss?" The guard called to her.

She stood. She had somehow managed to lightly doze. The clock on the wall read 3:15pm.

"He's ready for you. This way, please."

He opened a door for her and she walked through, following him down a long corridor. The fluorescent lights overhead flickered, threatening to quit altogether. Finally, they came upon a door, also locked. The guard swiped a card key and they went inside.

The room was long and rectangular with booths sitting against a thick pane of glass. All of the booths were empty except for a far one; the light overhead shone brightly and another stern-faced guard waited beside a chair, motioning her forward.

She took a deep breath, smoothed down the fabric of her skirt and walked forward. The guard put a gentle hand on her back and led her to a seat.

Across the pane of glass from her was a man.

She sat down, her eyes curious and studying him.

He had black hair, peppered with flecks of gray. His face was surprisingly smooth, freshly shaved. His eyes were blue, almost cerulean. Oddly familiar. He was very thin. The guard handed her a telephone receiver and she reluctantly held it to her ear.

The man studied her for a long time, a strange look in his blue eyes, and then slowly picked up his receiver as well.

No one said anything. Both just stared each other down for a long time, unsure of how to start the conversation.

Randall began. "They wanted me to look human walking out of here tomorrow, so..." he started, rubbing his smooth chin and cheeks thoughtfully.

Bree cleared her throat. "Do you remember me?"

He smiled broadly, showing a set of white teeth. "Of course, I do."

For a moment, her father's face flashed before her eyes. Weather-worn and torn down by age, Joseph Ward. The happy times that she had together with her parents. However brief a period that was.

Then the image of his crumpled body at the foot of the stairs. Her mother huddled in a corner, spouting craziness about a ninth stone.

A man walking down the stairs with black eyes.

This man.

This man.

Right in front of her.

Older now but the same person who met her gaze and smiled, a cool, vicious smile, a bloodied knife held tightly in his hand as he slowly came down the stairs.

"Do...do you remember what you did?" She hated the meek way that her voice came out. She wanted to be formidable, a worthy opponent. She wanted to growl at this man; she wanted to frighten him as badly as he had frightened her.

He didn't respond. His smile had completely vanished but now he just stared at her silently.

"How about the ninth stone? Do you know anything about that?"

His eyes narrowed.

"What did you say?"

"The ninth stone. My mom was muttering about it the night

you…" Her voice trailed off. She couldn't say the words. Even now, twenty years later, she was terrified to say it out loud. That her father had been murdered. Because saying something somehow made it more true.

He started to breathe heavy; his voice grew raspy and he was beginning to get physically agitated. A guard within his room started to walk towards him.

"The ninth stone? How could you possibly know…"

"What is it? What does that mean?"

"….no one knew…"

"Why did you do it? Why did you kill my father?!"

"…the beast… the black-eyed beast…"

"Why did you kill my father?!"

Her screams alerted the guards down the corridor and they began moving towards her as well.

"…go see Professor Hurley… he will tell you all…but I can't… you can't possibly know about the ninth stone…"

"I don't give a shit about any fucking stone! Tell me why you murdered my father!" Hot tears sprung to her cheeks; her face grew red. "Tell me!!"

A guard grabbed Randall around the waist and hoisted him up. He had suddenly turned into a worthless heap in his arms. Threw him to the ground. Put him in handcuffs.

Bree still held the telephone receiver tightly in her hands, her grip sweaty.

"Tell me why you did it, you fucking bastard!! Tell me!! You fucking coward! I hope you rot in hell! I hope you fucking rot!"

The guard placed a hand on her shoulder but she angrily shrugged it away. She watched as the guard led Randall out of the room, cuffed and bedraggled. Not at all the suave talker she had seen on television interviews.

Even after he was gone, Bree still held the receiver in her hand, now sobbing softly, her head slouched over in defeat. She had come here for an answer to one question.

And she had failed.

CHAPTER TWO
CARLISLE

Her phone was ringing.

Yet she was too tired to move. She was face down on her bed, arms flailed out to either side, and she didn't want to wake up.

Because if she woke up that would mean that she would have to face the day.

And she wasn't ready to do that yet.

A little while later her phone began to ring again; it was on her nightstand beside her and she pushed it off. It fell to the floor and went quiet.

A few moments later, her house phone began to ring. Bree opened her eyes.

No one knew her house phone number except for David and her Grandmother's nursing home. She started to move and threw her feet over the bed. The answering machine clicked on.

"This message is for Miss Adams. This is Mary from Sunshine Meadows nursing center; I'm calling in regards to your grandmother Doris. If you could please give us a call or come down to the nursing center, it would be appreciated. Thank you."

A cold chill ran down Bree's spine.

Something was wrong.

She threw the covers back and got up. Grabbed some discarded jeans from the floor and slid into them.

Her hair was a huge tangled mess; she grabbed an elastic and just threw it up. Put on her shoes. Grabbed her purse and keys. And she was out the door.

The incessant beeping.

It came from down the hall. The smell of piss and ammonia hung thick in the air. The women that milled around the hallways were impervious to the scent; they smiled and made their rounds.

Today was the same as the one before.

Each day the same routine.

The same drill. The same mundane tasks that needed to be accomplished. Medications to be given, bedpans to be changed, messes to be cleaned.

Each day as the one before.

Except for the woman sitting alone in the corner room.

Alone with a corpse.

Her neck hurt; how long had she sat this way? Hunched over and staring at the cheap speckled linoleum, her hand still clasped firmly to the cold, wrinkled arm. Now hardening, growing colder by the second. The arms that she had run into after losing her family. That embraced her as she cried. After her world went topsy-turvy.

How long had she been here?

A woman in scrubs in the corridor uttered a name to another: *Doris.* They looked towards her from the hallway, concerned. She didn't notice. Bree couldn't move. She couldn't bring herself to lift her head ever so slightly. To look upon that face one more time.

The beeping. Consistent and deep. It echoed hollowly through the hallway.

For the first time in a long time, her mind was clear.

Such clarity in such a moment terrified her. But there was a relief there, as much as she hated to admit it. She had lost everything. What more was there to ever worry about?

She hadn't cried. She couldn't cry. All she could do was stare at the floor, her eyes tracing slow patterns in the specks. Forming constellations, pictures.

Was there a man who created these speckles like an artist would wave a brush? Was he happy to know that his life's work was the sight of the underside of people's dirty feet, the terrible messes that older folks sometimes had, dribbling unspeakable things all over his creative vision? Did this make him proud?

She could sense someone watching her. A figure from the doorway cleared their throat. Bree finally lifted her head slightly, her neck crying out in pain.

One of the nurse's stood in the doorway, her hair off her face in a messy bun, her blue scrubs somehow spotless.

"Is there someone we can call, hon?" She asked Bree, shifting uncomfortably on her feet. For an establishment such as this, Bree thought it somehow comical at the girl's discomfort.

And yet her question brought a certainty crashing home. It hit her with such voracity that for a moment Bree had to remind herself to breathe. A violent little shudder rippled through her throat, tightening it and swelling it to the brink of tears. But she would not let them come.

She was alone.

"No," she finally croaked. "There's no one."

The nurse shifted again, looked over to Doris' corpse and walked away, conversing quietly with a man in the waiting room. After a moment he came over to the same doorway and spoke.

"I'm sorry, Miss. My name is Edward. I'm afraid I'm going to need to take a look at your..."

Bree sighed.

"My grandmother. She was my grandmother." Despite her best intentions, Bree's eyes strayed over to the unmoving form. And she was immediately assaulted with sorrow. It came rushing over her so richly that it was hard to breathe.

Doris' face was drawn, somehow shrunken, devoid of life. Her eyes were blessedly closed, her lips slightly parted, now useless pieces of cold flesh no longer harboring passing breath. Just a shell.

Edward came into the room slowly, trying to show his sympathy and compassion but also needing to do his job. The blonde nurse followed him, moving over to Bree while Edward moved over to Doris' body.

The nurse touched Bree's shoulder. It was meant to be a reassuring gesture, but it only felt cold to Bree. She was going through the motions. Through the required steps to get Bree out of the building and allow her to continue her rounds.

The beeping down the hallway continued to echo. Doesn't anyone check on their patients? Bree thought bitterly.

"Miss? Would you like a cup of coffee or tea?" Blondie was kneeling in front of Bree now, her hand lacing its way around Bree's.

It was again a movement that was meant to be bonding, a human connection. But to Bree it felt forced. Superficial. Insincere.

She wanted to spit venom at the woman, to hiss at her to leave her alone. And yet, despite her best efforts, she pitied the girl and looked up at her. Managed a wan smile.

"Yes. Tea would be nice, thank you."

She allowed the nurse to help her up from the chair and slowly move out of the room, as if she was the person most in need of assistance in an old age home.

Bree turned back just once to look upon the body of her grandmother, who Edward was tending to, getting ready to place in a body bag and send to the county morgue.

She anticipated a swell of sadness as she gazed upon her face. But she felt nothing.

Her grandmother was gone.

There was nothing left for her here.

She didn't want to go home. Somehow the apartment would seem emptier without Doris. Everything suddenly seemed emptier without Doris.

She called David. Told him what happened. They met at The Bean.

His arms surrounded her in a hug and she collapsed against him, thankful for his presence. But she did not cry. She couldn't.

They sat down and ordered a couple of coffees and a piece of chocolate cake that Bree picked at mindlessly with her fork.

"I'm so sorry, Bree. Whatever you need help with, planning the funeral, I'm here."

"I just... I can't believe she's gone. I feel so terrible because I haven't seen her in weeks. I've been so consumed with work that I didn't make it over there to visit."

He put a hand over hers. "I'm sure she knew that you loved her."

She pulled her hand away and let the fork fall to her plate.

"It's not just that, Davey. She was... she was all that I had in the world. Grandma was...home to me. Now she's gone. And I don't have anyone."

He grabbed her hand and held onto it tightly, despite her attempt to pull away. She gave up and looked at him as he told her, "That's not true."

His eyes were diverted over her shoulder and suddenly his face grew pale. David's mouth slacked open in soundless shock.

"What? Davey, what's wrong?" She squeezed his hand.

"Holy shit." And he got up, walked past her without another word.

Bree turned in her seat and watched him move over to the TV hanging on the wall, reached up and turned up the volume. The few customers in the coffee shop were entranced by the news story as well.

It was the byline ticker running under the blonde reporter's face that made her blood run cold. Her mouth dropped open, tiny hairs on the back of her neck standing on end.

The din of the restaurant grew silent as the reporter's message echoed through the coffee shop.

"Again, for those just joining the broadcast, it has been confirmed that convicted murderer Randall Carlisle, who was slated for release this morning, was found dead in his cell. The incident is still under investigation. Reports confirm that he was visited yesterday by none other than Miss Breanna Ward, daughter of the slain victim Joseph Ward. Sources confirm that Carlisle grew agitated and his distress may have led to his suicide. More questions than answers have come up in this strange story; why would a man hang himself only hours before he was scheduled to be released from prison? What exactly did Miss Ward say to him? We have been unable to reach Miss Ward for a statement."

"Oh my God..." Bree whispered quietly as she saw David turn towards her, questions in his eyes. There was a commotion outside and Bree saw a number of vans pull up suddenly, parking in the middle of the street. Floods of cameramen and reporters merged onto the sidewalk of The Bean.

Rachel, the barista behind the counter, saw the throng of people and moved over to Bree and David.

"Shit, you guys better get out of here. There's an employee entrance in the back. Go!" She said and flew over to the front door to fight off the incoming reporters.

Bree and David ran down a small back hallway, a sink and coatrack with aprons and jackets and a timeclock with employee timesheets hanging on the wall. They came upon a door with a green Exit sign illuminating above and David burst through it, sunshine immediately flooding into Bree's eyes.

The back alley was empty; the reporters hadn't had a chance to make their way around to it yet. But they both knew they didn't have a lot of time.

"Come on, B," David said to her and grabbed her hand. They ran north through the alley towards Spring Street. Her legs kept pumping harder and harder until she felt like her lungs would explode. They could hear the rising murmur of the sounds of voices overlapping. Bree turned back briefly and saw a number of reporters flow out the back of The Bean and come after her.

"Shit, Davey, how the hell do they know who I am?" Bree asked, turning back around and trying to keep up with David's long strides.

"I have no idea. But reporters are tenacious. They're like a dog with a bone; once they get a taste of something they like, they rip it apart to the marrow. It was really only a matter of time, B," he said, almost breathless.

Up ahead, they saw an Uber parked on the side of Spring Street. David threw up a hand to the driver who was sitting in the front seat staring at a cell phone. He glanced up and gave him a nod.

They were in the back of the Uber and driving away when the news vans turned the corner of Spring Street and began to follow them. The throng of reporters, their cameramen in tow, were still running to catch up from behind the strip mall.

Bree held her hand up to her chest, trying to catch her breath.

"Where to?" The Uber driver asked, eyeing the two of them in the backseat with a fair amount of suspicion.

"B, you can't go home. Come and stay at my apartment for the night. They'll be camped outside your place."

She just nodded silently in reply. Her brain was still trying to process, still trying to figure out what she had just learned. What had just happened. Not only was the media and the world now aware of who she was, she was grappling to come to terms with the fact that Carlisle was dead. Killed himself just hours before he was set to be released.

Why would he do that? What had she said that distressed him so?

The vans trailing her, filled to the brim with reporters, eager to get the scoop on the hottest story of the decade, were going to pound her with that very question.

She found irony in the fact that she herself had no idea what the answer was to that question.

"East Village," he told the driver and sat back, his arms reaching around Bree's shoulders. "You okay?"

She just nodded mutely, not sure how to answer that.

Her office knew who she was now, she was sure of it. If the news had already caught onto her identity, she was sure that Veronica and all of her colleagues were gobsmacked with amazement. And would only treat her with delicacy from this point forward, which was something she was hoping to avoid.

It was a terrible moment in her life. But it was a moment. One that she did not wish to have define her. She didn't want to live in that moment, languish there forever. Bree changed her name, not out of shame, but out of a genuine desire to live a normal life.

The Uber driver made a few superfluous turns to try to shake the tail of vans that were following them, and once he was certain he lost them, he finally pulled in front of David's building.

David had a cup of tea in front of her within a few minutes of reaching his apartment. He held it out to her as she sat down on the worn, black leather sofa.

Bree smiled up at him wanly. "Thank you."

He sat down next to her on the sofa, a cold beer in his hand. David was the first to say anything.

"What a shitty day," he simply said, taking a long swig of his cold Budweiser.

"Amen to that," she replied, blowing the steam off the top of her tea and slowly taking a drink.

"I mean, first your poor grandmother. Then what the fuck happened to Randall? And now you've been made. Everyone in New York, no, the entire world knows who you are. Where you are.

What you've been through. And they want to find you, hunt you down, pick at your bleeding scars just to make fucking TV ratings."

Bree choked back a silent sob and nodded. Another sip of tea.

He stood up, paced the small space of his living room angrily, like a panther prowling a cage. She could tell that he was upset, angry, frustrated for her. But her mind was still trying to process everything that had just happened in the space of the last half hour. Everything that she just learned. And until she was able to do that, she thought silence was the only recourse.

"Bree, you need to get out of here for a while. After your grandmother's funeral, you just need to run. Get out for a few weeks until all of this craziness dies down." David finished off his beer and put the empty bottle on top of the fireplace mantel.

He knelt down in front of her, took her cup away, placed it on the table, and grabbed both of her small hands in his.

"Bree. Hey, look at me."

Her eyes slowly obeyed.

"You need to leave. Let me help you make the funeral arrangements and then get the hell out of Dodge for a while, okay? Give them a few weeks and this will all die down a bit. I promise you." He told her, his light brown eyes genuine.

Again, she was suddenly assailed with a deep feeling of aloneness. Where in the world would she go?

"Peru," she said finally, the first word she had said since running from the coffee shop. It came to her from out of nowhere. She just seemed to snatch it out of the sky, grab at it and cling to it as if that's the only place in the world where she could go.

David was a little surprised at the abruptness of his idea taking hold. But he smiled.

"Peru? You want to go to Peru?"

"Will you come with me?"

His eyes darkened a little bit. "I can't, Bree. I have that summit for work that I need to prepare for. I really wish I could."

She was afraid she might be hit with another wave of loneliness, but this time, with Peru in the forefront of her mind, it passed. Didn't have a chance to take hold. With or without David, whatever she needed in Peru awaited her. She had a mission. A place to go.

It filled her with the oddest feeling. A chill, one that was riven with suspicion and dread began to fill her heart, but in a very dark moment of helplessness and despair, she had a mission. She had a destination. And that was all she wanted in the world.

"Davey, do you believe in fate?" She asked him, her voice sudden and meek.

Again, he sat back for a moment, surprised. "Why do you ask that, B?"

She sat there for a moment, her eyes clearing from what appeared to be a strange fog. Bree shook her head.

"Nevermind." She said simply, reaching out and finishing off her tea.

"Okay. Tomorrow I'll reach out to the funeral parlor and take care of the arrangements. And then Peru. But right now, right now I need sleep," she said.

David nodded in silent understanding, standing up and grabbing a blanket for himself from a hall closet. Before he had a chance to offer his bedroom, Bree was already stretched out on the worn-down sofa, eyes closed. He smiled and covered her up with the blanket, turned off the lights and went to his bedroom.

David awoke in the middle of the night, not sure what roused him. He glanced over at the clock on his bedside table.

3:13am.

He sat up in his bed, the hairs on his arm rising. David sniffed the air; he could smell something burning.

Alarmed, he threw his feet over the side of the bed and stood up. It was a slight smell, not very strong. He wasn't entirely sure if it was even coming from his apartment or another.

He opened his bedroom door and peeked out into the living room. The smell of burning was much stronger; his eyes ran over to the sofa and a cold chill ran through him.

Bree was gone.

David threw a T-shirt over his head and called out to the dark apartment, "Bree?"

He went to the bathroom to see if she was inside, but the door stood open, the light off, empty.

A cold shiver ran the length of his spine.

Something was wrong.

"B? B, where are you?" He called to the apartment, moving into the kitchen, his eyes even checking underneath the table. David went back to his bedroom, turned on the lights, the harsh glare repugnant to his eyes at such an early hour. But she wasn't in his room either.

"Bree? Where are you?" His voice called out, getting more shrill. He hated how scared he sounded. But where could she be?

He saw the door to his apartment was slightly ajar. Another cold ripple moved through him.

Maybe she'd decided to go back to her apartment after all, he told himself. But she certainly would have left him a note at the very least.

He opened the door and peered out into the dimly lit hallway. There, wedged in the door leading to the roof, was the blanket.

"Fuck!" He ran down the hallway, threw open the door and ran up the stairs to the roof as fast as he could. A million thoughts were running through his head at that moment, the smell of burning even more potent in the empty stairwell. He was worried she might have jumped, despondent over everything that had happened that day.

But that smell. That burning smell with nothing burning...

He threw open the door and the cool night air hit him harshly.

"Bree!" He called out, turned, and saw her.

She stood near the edge of the building rooftop, her back to him. She made no motion or gave any indication of having heard him.

He approached her slowly.

"Bree, let's talk about this, okay?" He tried to make his voice as light as possible. He didn't want to antagonize her. He wanted himself to appear to be incredibly calm.

She didn't move. Only stood standing at the edge of the rooftop, her back to him. If she heard him call her name, she gave no sign.

"B? I'm here. You have someone who cares about you. I will always be here for you," he whispered to her softly as he finally reached her, walked around the side of her, trying to put himself between her and the edge of the rooftop.

What he saw horrified him.

Her gaze was blank. Staring out in silence over the din of late-night car traffic and far-off sounds of sirens.

She had one of her sleeves rolled up, blood dripping down in slow but steady blobs of crimson at her feet. David saw she had a knife in her hand; she had carved what looked like an upside-down crucifix on her forearm.

But it wasn't the blank stare. Or the macabre primitive tattoo she had just given herself.

The thing that made David terrified was her eyes.

He couldn't tell for sure in the darkness of the night… but he could swear that her eyes were black.

His hand reached out and slowly took the knife from her right hand, threw it to the ground out of her reach.

"Bree? Bree, are you okay?" His hands went on her shoulders, again, his voice soft and calm.

Nothing. She stood staring at him in silence.

"Bree! Bree, wake up!" He yelled a bit louder this time, his hands shaking her shoulders.

Her eyes flipped shut. When she opened them, they were her normal hue, confused and glancing around warily at her surroundings.

She winced and then looked down at her forearm.

"Oh my God… what the fuck?" She cried out as she saw it, the mutilation she had done to herself. "Davey! What happened?"

Relieved, he hugged her briefly, and then led her back to his apartment.

This time, he guided her into his bedroom. Sat her on the edge of his bed. He went to the bathroom and found some alcohol and bandages. Cleaned up her arm as best he could. Thankfully not deep enough for stitches, but she would forever have a scar.

Bree bent over in sobs, finally breaking free from her like a bubbling spring. He put his arm around her, pulling her closer to him. David couldn't tell if these were tears of sadness from the day, or if they were tears of terror from the night.

But he had to ask the question.

He pulled away from her for a moment, using his hand to tilt her head towards him. Forcing her to meet his gaze.

"Bree, you were on the roof. Standing on the edge. With a knife in your hand. Did you… were you planning to…"

"No!" She cried. "At least, I… I don't think so… I don't remember, Davey. I don't remember anything. I fell asleep on the sofa and the next thing I know you're shaking me awake on the roof."

"Okay. Okay," he said, his hand stroking her hair.

"What is going on, Davey? What happened?" She asked him, her eyes desperate and red from crying. Bree was terrified. And he was anguished at not being able to help his friend, to do or say something for her that would give her some peace.

"I don't know, B. I just don't know." That was all that he could muster. And it fell remarkably short. But for whatever reason, she seemed to relax. It might have been his arm around her, his fingers running through her long hair. Or it could have been just sheer exhaustion.

"Bree, lie back," he instructed her. She did, and he pulled the covers around her, fluffed a pillow for her head. He crawled into the bed next to her.

Their relationship had been strictly platonic from the first outset of their meeting. David had hoped that might change one day. He couldn't lie and say that he never noticed how beautiful she was, and he couldn't deny that her beauty was the reason why he approached her at the coffee shop in the first place the day they met. It was simply that when they started talking, he felt a kinship with her that he was hesitant to tarnish or perhaps destroy with anything romantic.

He loved Bree. She was his best friend. And, at the current moment, he was the only thing she had left in the world. His honor and morality wouldn't let him destroy that for her.

But as he crawled into bed with her, and she so easily went to him, drowned in his arms, melting closely into him, her fingers curled against his back... he tried with all of his might to fight the temptation.

What she needed right now was comfort. Support. And he would be that for her, for as long as she wanted him to.

Instead, his lips brushed the top of her apricot-scented head and kissed her.

Another night…

Another night…

The funeral was sparsely attended, save for the throng of chattering news reporters that were lining the road near the parking lot. Most of her grandmother's friends had already passed away. Bree stood by the graveside in her black shift, staring down awkwardly at the coffin as it was lowered into the ground.

She felt self-conscious. The people that were in attendance looked to her sympathetically, anticipating a reaction. And yet Bree was not the type to broadcast her emotions. She couldn't wait for this to be over.

A warm hand laced through her fingers and she turned. David was there, smiling faintly at her, his eyes encouraging. She was appreciative that he came.

As the coffin was lowered, the priest recited a Bible verse, meant to bring comfort to loved ones. Bree felt a sudden chill; she looked up and off across the cemetery.

There was a woman standing near a small enclave of trees. She wore a long, dark dress.

She stared at Bree silently, her eyes somehow empty. And then she smiled.

Bree looked away, disturbed by her presence. Was she a friend of Grandmother's? She thought to herself. She grasped David's hand tighter, and he squeezed hers twice in response.

"...and God shall wipe away all tears from their eyes; and there shall be no more death, neither sorrow, nor crying, neither shall there by any more pain; for the former things are passed away."

Bree looked up as the priest droned on. The woman was still standing where she had been, continuing her cold stare at Bree. Her eyes looked empty.

The smile remained transfixed on her face and yet it had somehow changed. It had been a cold smile, nothing behind it. But now it looked maniacal. Insane.

Murderous.

Bree nudged David slightly, her eyes never leaving the woman's disturbing face.

"Who is that lady?" She whispered to him.

David looked up, glanced around the cemetery.

"What lady?"

For a brief second Bree broke her gaze and looked to David incredulously. "Are you kidding me? The lady right th..."

When she turned back, the woman was gone.

The reception that followed the service was an endless procession of guests hugging Bree, expressing their sympathy, telling her how wonderful a person her Grandmother Doris was. How much Doris had loved her. How dearly Doris would be missed.

Bree felt nothing but irritation; they were speaking about her

Grandmother as if they knew her best. They didn't know her as well as Bree did. But she smiled and thanked them for coming.

The reporters were still camped outside her grandmother's house, biding their time. After the graveside service, they hit her with the force of a storm gale as she approached her car.

"Breanna!! What did you say to Randall to make him kill himself? What did you say? Breanna, did you want Randall to die? Breanna, what happened the night your parents died?"

All of the memories, all of the questions forced her to relieve them all over again. Over and over and over. Which was why she wanted to become an Adams. And leave Ward behind forever.

But her thoughts never strayed far from the woman she had seen in the cemetery. There was something off about her. Something not quite right.

Her eyes had turned almost completely black; and that smile was not an inviting one.

After the reception, she and David cleaned up slowly. The house her Grandmother had lived in before she went into the nursing home was largely left untouched for years. Paid off by her Grandfather Harold before he had passed away a decade before. It sat empty on the street, a ghost of her childhood spent running through the halls, collecting dust.

"All things considered, Bree, it was a nice ceremony."

All things considered. Bree chuckled mildly and looked up at him. His brown eyes were twinkling. He knew how she felt about church and religion. But it was important to her Grandmother. Doris had been a devout Catholic until the day she died.

"Thanks, Davey. I'm sure she would have appreciated the effort." She said, throwing a half-empty plastic cup of punch in the garbage bag she carried around.

"I was pretty sure you were going to bolt at the graveside so I thought it best to hold onto you," David said, his voice still teasing. "Why'd you get so skittish anyway? That was a little beyond, even for you."

"Ha ha," she replied sarcastically, shoving a paper plate with a half-eaten piece of cake into her bag. Why they serve cake at a funeral she never understood. Cakes were usually symbolized to celebrate something. And her Grandmother's death was not something she felt like celebrating.

"Did you really not see that lady?" She asked him, standing up and staring at him quizzically.

David laughed. "Breanna, I think you're off your rocker. You've always been one to get cagey in cemeteries and stuff. So, you figure you'd mess with me at the most inappropriate moment to do so. Typical, B."

Her smile slowly faded.

"Davey, I wouldn't do that. Not at my Grandmother's funeral. You really didn't see her?"

David looked up, the merriment draining from his face.

"No. Bree, are you alright?"

Bree was puzzled but shook it off and managed a faint smile. "Yeah, yeah, I'm fine. Let's just get this place cleaned up and order some food. I don't really feel like going into the city tonight."

David nodded silently and helped her clear the rest of the trash.

A few hours later they were sitting on the sofa, half of a devoured pizza on the coffee table. Bree had a box of pictures on her lap, and she laughed and smiled as she picked through them all.

Doris as a baby. Doris as a little girl, skinned knees and muddy hands, snot dripping down her chin. Prom night, a sensible long dress and a handsome date on her arm. Her wedding; Grandpa Harold's wide smile beaming, showing off an almost oddly perfect set of white teeth. He was just as she remembered, albeit much younger. And Doris, her small white pillbox hat with a short netting that made up her veil. Standing in front of a small cake with rose trim, her new husband by her side. Smiling as if she had not a care in the world. Their wedding looked like it had been a small affair. Intimate. Modest.

Typical Doris. She was not one for pomp, flash or fanfare. She lived a quiet, happy life with her husband. Gardening. Cooking. Looking after her granddaughter. Bridge nights with her friends.

Bree's throat tightened a bit and she could feel the tears coming; the familiar light in her grandmother's eyes was too much. The house seemed colder; emptier. Quieter. What had once been a bustling home filled with warmth and the wafting smells of her Grandmother's baking was now vacant. Harsh. Almost callous.

Memories hung in the air but they were mere shadows of their former selves. They haunted the place with their faded happiness, reminding Bree that they were forever gone. That things would never be the same.

"Oh, look! Isn't this you?" David cried, grabbing a small photo from the box. He held it up and smiled.

Bree smiled too. She hadn't seen the photo in decades. She was around eight years old, standing on the sidewalk in front of the house. Her best friend Solveig stood at her side, her pigtails messily braided on either side of her face. Bree's black hair was unkempt as well, knotted up and plastered with sweat to the side of her face. Her light brown eyes danced giddily. The girls held each other close in the picture and smiled broadly. They always loved hamming it up for the camera.

"Oh, God, Solveig! I haven't thought about her in years!" Bree chuckled to herself, her finger tracing over the picture lovingly. "She was my best friend in the world. My only real friend growing up. She lived right down the street in that yellow house. We were joined at the hip. For a while, anyway."

David grabbed the picture back and studied it. "You look like a little homeless in this picture." He laughed.

"Shut up!" She elbowed him playfully. "My grandma always brushed my hair perfectly in the morning and I'd always come in disheveled, like I had just gotten done fighting a monster. Eventually she realized I was a lost cause. She came to terms with the fact that I was a tomboy just like my Mom..."

Bree's voice trailed off and her eyes grew dark. David noticed and sighed softly.

"Does she know?" He asked her.

Bree nodded.

"Have you seen her?" He continued.

Bree shook her head. "The orderly told her."

David shook his head slowly. "How long has it been, Bree? Don't you think you ought to…"

"No." She replied firmly. From the sound of her voice, David knew not to press the issue. His gaze drifted back to the picture of Bree as a child. His eyes narrowed.

"Who is that?" He asked.

"Who is what?"

"That? Who the hell is that?" He asked, motioning to the picture.

She turned to him and followed his gaze.

At first, she didn't see what he was referring to. She saw both young girls smiling goofily at the camera, living up the carefree summer day, oblivious to anything except their own little world. But behind them there was a shadow.

Further off down the street, standing next to a large hedge that edged a lawn, was the shape of a man.

Bree's eyes narrowed too, moving closer to the picture, hoping to pick out any distinguishing characteristics, to get a clear view of the face.

But it was only a shadow. Too far away to pick out anything clearly. The shadow just stood by the hedge, staring at the two girls.

Her grandmother had taken the picture. Surely she must have seen him.

"Do you see it? It looks like someone's standing there watching you." David said, pointing out what was so obvious to her now she could hardly imagine not seeing it before.

Bree shook her head, incredulous. "I have seen this picture dozens of times. Hundreds of times, probably. And I've never seen this before."

David saw the fear on her face. First the woman in the cemetery, now this strange figure in an old picture. David smiled and laughed lightly. "It's probably just a neighbor passing by. That's all."

And before she had a moment to protest, he thrust the picture back deep into the box, buried underneath all the other pictures from a lifetime ago.

She was led into a small room. A diminutive man in a gray suit sat at a table and stared at her intensely when she entered. He was balding and very stone-faced.

"Breanna?" He asked, reading briefly from a fat file folder in front of him.

"Yes," she responded quietly, sitting down in the hardback chair and waited. She had come all the way back down to the prison based on a phone call. The halls still echoed with Randall's footsteps. A cold chill ran across her neck at the thought.

"I understand this is an extremely difficult time. And after thoroughly reading the case file, I have a pretty good understanding of your history with Randall Carlisle."

She nodded silently, patiently, waiting.

"We're all quite taken aback by what's happened. Randall always had a generous and optimistic nature to him; over the years he became quite liked amongst the other prisoners and even the staff." The man balked suddenly and straightened his back.

"I apologize. That was insensitive."

"Yes. It was." She was in no mood for polite frivolities.

He cleared his throat awkwardly and opened up the case file again, sifting through papers. It struck her then that this gentleman seemed to be even more nervous than she was.

"I understand you came to see Randall the day that he... took his life." The gentleman was all business again, stern faced and solemn.

Breanna nodded silently. She made no inclination that she wanted anything more from him than the punchline. The entire experience had been a circus that she longed to put behind her.

"We were a little concerned about something that we found on him when he... when he passed. It was a note. And it was addressed to you."

Breanna's blood ran cold and her heart began to beat rapidly within her chest. She felt like her stomach was in her throat.

"Me?"

"Yes. You. Look..." He took off his wiry glasses and set them on the table, rubbing the bridge of his nose between his fingers. For a moment his pretenses were down. His business demeanor had vanished. He took on a personal tone.

"Here's the thing. We have an educated, well-learned man who is a convicted murderer. He did his time, behaved and was set to be released within a matter of hours. And then after a visit from you, he goes back to his cell and hangs himself with his bedsheet, a note addressed to you clasped in his cold hand. Not a goodbye note to his dearly loved wife or children. But you. A girl who he had not seen for years. And an ambiguous message that has all of us here at the station scratching our heads. His wife would like some resolution, as you can understand. But instead all we have is this."

From the file folder he brought out a crumpled piece of paper. Reluctantly he pushed it across the table towards her. She sat staring at it awkwardly for a moment, refusing to touch it. Instead she crossed her arms defiantly and slunk down a bit in her chair.

"His wife wants resolution. His wife. I'm sure my mother would like some resolution as well. But I bet you haven't thought much about her since your precious Randall has been behaving so well and charming the guards. You fail to remember that this educated, well learned family man decided to sneak into a stranger's house in the middle of the night and murder a beloved husband and father. For a reason that remains a mystery to this day. An action that made a basket case out of my mother and a fucking mess out of me. The way I see it, Mr.... whoever you are, whatever your name is. I really don't care. In this life, you create your own resolution. No one gets it for free."

She stood up from the chair, causing it to crash behind her, grabbed the grubby, crumpled note and walked out the door.

In the safety of her car, her hands shaking, she opened up the note. Scrawled in an almost child-like handwriting, written in the final moments of a man's life, were the words:

NOTHING IS AS IT SEEMS, BREANNA.

I'M SORRY.

R

CHAPTER THREE
PERU

It took only a few weeks for her grandmother's house to sell. Though it sold for at least $20,000 less than what it was worth, Bree was happy to have the task done. It was hard to do; her grandmother's house was the only happy place from her childhood. But it was an obligation that she had to take care of. After she returned from Peru, she still had to go through the daunting task of cleaning it out in time for the new owners to take possession.

Doris had left everything to her only granddaughter in her will. Including the revenue from the sale of the home. It wasn't much, but it was enough to take some of the strain off Bree's shoulders as she tried to piece her life back together. Luckily work kept her occupied, keeping her mind from wandering.

Things had been as awkward as she anticipated when she returned to work. Everyone gave her a pretty wide berth and she would catch them whispering and glancing in her direction. But at the very least, the security in the office meant that the reporters that had been hounding her would be forced to stay away. It was one good thing to cling to at a time like this.

David had been a great friend to her; he had always been there. He was a nice change from the usual self-absorbed people that she encountered in Manhattan. He was real; he reminded her of the people she grew up with in Bantam. David was like a breath of fresh air.

The loudspeaker crackled to life, and she heard the attendant's voice announce that her plane was boarding for Peru. She grabbed her luggage and ticket and went to stand in line at the counter, eager to take off.

Escaping New York for a few weeks away was the last thing on Bree's mind as she now had a house full of furniture to sell off.

David had brought over a bottle of wine to her apartment the night before she left, mentioning that his brother recently came back from Peru and had amazing pictures. Knowing her love of history and architecture, he figured it would be an obvious choice for a quick escape. He was championing her, always her stalwart cheerleader. He thought Peru would do wonders for her.

She felt like she was balancing on the tip of a pin; that there was still much to resolve, much to tie up before it would really hit her. That her grandmother was truly gone. And until then, taking a trip away just seemed like the last thing she should be doing.

But David was insistent.

"Breanna, you've always done what you *should* do. I know this is what your grandmother would have wanted. She wanted you to live, to enjoy your life. You're holding on too tightly to the past and the things that have happened to you. I think this would be a great fresh start to a new chapter for you. I really do. By the time you get back to New York, everyone will have forgotten about Randall Carlisle."

Eventually she relented. And before she knew it, her travel agent had presented her with one roundtrip ticket to South America.

David could not afford to take the time away from work and

refused to let her pay his way. He insisted that a journey on her own would be good for the soul.

And so it was that she found herself sitting in a crowded airport terminal at JFK, snacking on a small bag of trail mix and watching the rain fall beyond the windows. Waiting for a plane to take her on her next big adventure.

"Damas y caballeros, llegaremos a Peru en 20 minutos. Ladies and gentlemen, we will be arriving to Peru in 20 minutes." The flight attendant's voice rang out over the intercom.

Bree took off her headphones and turned off her iPod, shoving it back into the bag at her feet. Her eyes turned to the window.

Lima was a small scattering of low buildings, littered in almost a haphazard way across the landscape. The sky was gray and foreboding, sheer cliffs on the coast dropping off to an angry sea. She shifted her eyes slightly and saw a large mass in the center of town. Curious, she peered a bit closer to the glass.

The gentleman sitting next to her noticed her interest. "That is Huaca Pucllana. It is an ancient shrine. A sacred place." His accent was thick and she guessed he was a local returning home.

"A shrine? In the middle of the city?" She asked, her eyes narrowing in confusion.

He laughed. "Si. You turista?"

"Yes. Is it that obvious?" She grinned, bemused.

He laughed again. "Si. You from New York?"

She stared at him sideways for a moment, suspicious. "How did you know that?"

"Ah, all Americans are from New York, no?"

This time she smiled and laughed dryly. "Not all, no."

He held out a small hand. "Me llamo Jose."

She grinned and accepted. "My name is Bree. It's nice to meet you."

The moment their hands touched, a dark shadow passed over the man's features. He pulled away quickly, averted his eyes, looking troubled.

It was such a fluid, rapid action, Bree felt it was not something worth commenting on. But it bothered her. It was almost as if he suddenly saw something in her that scared him.

She shook her head slightly and turned back to the window quietly, her eyes drifting once more over the rolling buildings that made up urban Lima.

Bree's hotel was in the Miraflores district in Lima, right on the coast. Her room overlooked the rough and choppy, angry Pacific waters below the cliffs. She was surprised by the gray cloud cover and vicious looking ocean. Bree had this image in her mind that Peru would be tropical with calm seas.

It didn't break her stride. She'd heard of a fantastic restaurant in the Miraflores district that offer a 28-course tasting menu, ranked one of the top restaurants in the world. She quickly unpacked a few things and threw on a light pink shift dress and a pair of nude heels.

The restaurant was very high brow with decadent dishes that were passed on to her by gourmet chefs. Rich and delicious samplings of rabbit and beef tongue and caviar, dressed in things that she had never heard of before, paired with some exquisite wine.

By the time she got back to her hotel, she was exhausted. The flight, the long dinner, and the full tummy helped her fall asleep quickly that night.

But she didn't stay asleep for long...

She jolted awake, her body sitting bolt upright before her mind even knew why. Bree smelled something but couldn't quite place it.

She looked around the room, the unfamiliar shadows of furniture draped against the sable darkness, wondering where she was.

Peru.

She sniffed the air again, catching a glance at the bedside clock. It was a little after 3am. Something smelled foul, almost like cat urine. Potent and very strong in her room.

Why hadn't she smelled it before?

She got out of bed, knelt down at the duvet cover and smelled it. Nothing.

Confused, she rubbed the sleep out of her eyes, the scar on her arm suddenly sparking to life and burning. She looked down and saw that it had started to bleed again.

Frustrated, she figured she must have agitated it getting out of bed. Bree went to the bathroom to wash the blood away. Turned on the faucet, let it run a minute before the water warmed up, and then looked up at her reflection in the mirror.

She wasn't alone.

Behind her, there was a figure, a shadowy shape of what looked like a man in a cloak. The light in the bathroom was still off, and maybe it was her mind playing tricks on her, she thought to herself.

Quickly, she flipped the light on.

A sharp bright fluorescent light snapped on, and whatever was there was gone. The only thing she saw in the mirror was her own disheveled, confused reflection.

Curiosity got the better of her. Slowly, her finger strayed back over to the light switch, her heart suddenly pumping fresh blood. Fear gripped her spine but she just had to see…

She flipped the light off again.

The figure was back, and this time, much closer to her than before. The cloak was heavy and brown, deeply drawn so that Bree couldn't see his face. But she didn't need to.

She knew who this was.

Just then, she felt two gnarled hands close around her throat. She tried to let out a scream but her air was cut off as the fingers squeezed tighter. Bree's hands flailed out in front of her, scrambling to find something, anything to fight this creature off.

Her hands, as desperately as they wanted to move to her throat and fight the fingers off her throat, just couldn't bring themselves to do it. If she touched those gnarled fingers, that haunted her for years in her dreams, then it would mean he's real.

Despite the fact that he was right behind her, strangling her to death, somehow the touch of his fingers on hers would be paramount. And she inherently knew it.

Instead, after finding nothing useful to fight him off near the sink, her hands desperately reached back out for the light switch.

The fingers around her throat tightened even more, and she felt like he might crush her neck entirely. Panicked, desperate, her fingers brushed the light switch, praying, hoping, despairing that once she turned the light on again, he would vanish as he did before.

After one long moment that seemed to last a lifetime, Bree's finger finally reached the switch and she flipped it up.

The lights flashed on again.

Immediately, the pressure around her throat was gone. She fell to the ground, clutching at her neck, coughing and wheezing air into her empty lungs.

She felt the sobs rising up but they refused to come. Her body's immediate sole purpose was to try to find air, not elicit cries. Bree's eyes flew up to the empty bathroom, red and bloodshot from what had just transpired.

The man.

The man.

The man…

She had seen him before.

Once.

A very long time ago.

Scrambling to her feet, unsteady and tripping over herself, she ran through the hotel room, flipping on every light that she could. She threw herself down on the bed, already feeling her throat starting to swell and bruise.

The sobs came then. In the hotel room when she was alone, thousands of miles away from the only person she considered family.

The loss hit her yet again, like another wave bashing against an already exhausted ship.

Alone.

She was alone.

No change of venue, no new country was going to change that fact. Dealing with the loss of her grandmother was going to hurt in Peru just as much as in New York, possibly more so. Being away from David was more than she could stand.

That was the first time she felt the desire. The strong desire to end it all.

She grabbed her phone. Texted David to see if he was awake.

He was.

"Hey B, how's Peru?"

Bree sighed deeply. She texted back, "Good. Miss you."

She couldn't bring herself to tell him what had just happened. All she needed at that moment was to know that he was there.

That he was alive.

That he existed.

She sobbed then, the sobs ripping out of her tender, swollen throat viciously. She couldn't hold them in anymore.

Eventually, exhausted, Bree drifted back off to sleep, the lights all around her blazing. Before oblivion set in, she caught a slight, faint whiff of jasmine.

In the back of her mind, she knew that something was about to change. This man had haunted her since she was a little girl, yet tonight was the first time he touched her.

Harmed her.

Though she knew he always wanted to.

Just like she knew, deep within in her heart, that this was just the beginning...

The air in the catacombs smelled odd. It had a dank odor that reminded Bree of rotten things, of old, ancient, dusty things that had long since breathed. She was not in a place of life.

The short Peruvian gentleman looked to her, noticed her hesitation, and then spoke to her briefly in Spanish, urging her towards the open maw of the catacombs.

She crept forward, ducking down substantially to fit her frame in the small opening. She drew the scarf around her swollen, bruised neck a bit tighter, self-conscious. Bree found herself on a small catwalk held above deep embankments on either side. They were dimly lit and she made the grim mistake of looking over the edge.

There, about ten feet down, was a skeleton. The burial shroud had long ago withered away, but the white skeleton was well preserved. Smiling up at her with teeth that were gnarled and rotten. She looked questioningly at the gentleman and he explained to her, in broken English, that these were men of renown. They were given the honor of being buried separate from the rest of the monks. Putting a light hand on the small of her back, he urged her deeper onto the catwalk and into the depths of the catacombs. There was another entrance, shorter and smaller, and she went first.

The first thing she noticed was the heat. It was abnormally warm. Cramped. Little air. She thought once she had arrived it would have been cool, dark, damp. But it was nothing like that. She found herself standing on the precipice of a large platform in a circle room. Below, she once again looked down and saw something that gave her a chill, despite the warmth of the catacombs.

Hundreds, possibly thousands, of skulls littered the floor of this round antechamber. Small recessions were made in the wall, more skulls smiling out at her from within them. Long femur bones were arranged in a circle formation, the skulls making several rings around this bizarre and macabre circle.

"What..." She began, suddenly feeling a deep chill.

"This is one of several ossuaries in the convent. They stopped burying people here back in 1808," the guide told her. "They built the large cemetery right outside of the city after that and used that for burials. But it was rumored that this convent had tunnels that led directly to the nearby Tribunal of the Holy Inquisition."

"Inquisition? You mean the Spanish Inquisition?"

The guide shook his head somberly. "No. The Peruvian

Inquisition. It began about 100 years after the Spanish Inquisition and lasted for centuries. It was a very dark and deadly time for Peru."

Bree turned to him, intrigued. "What happened exactly?"

The guide ran a hand over his balding head and looked morose as he began. "The Catholic church had a far reach back in those days. Many Europeans who refused to convert fled to avoid religious persecution and ended up in Lima. When the Inquisition began, they were tortured, mutilated… and finally killed. No one knows for sure how many people were killed during those days. A lot of Jewish immigrants and Protestants fled to Peru, hoping for a better life. But it eventually caught up to them."

Bree looked down at the countless skulls, no markers, no identifiers. Just nameless bones, anonymous ash. She felt her heart well with a pang of deep sadness.

"What exactly did they do to them?" She asked, almost afraid to hear the answer.

The guide looked just as uncomfortable talking about it in such a sacred place, but ultimately he knew if he made her happy, there would be a big tip.

He cleared his throat. "Stocks for days upon end, toca, or more aptly known as waterboarding, the rack, burning the bottoms of the feet. Ultimately if they did not confess to heresy, they were burned at the stake. Their ashes and bones left to rot and fester here. Forever unmarked and unremembered."

"That's awful. They would just pull anyone off the street and declare them to be a heretic?" She asked.

"Not just anyone. They were more than likely either Jewish or Muslim, or recent *conversos*. Conversos were people who had recently converted to Catholicism, and they were eyed with a great deal of suspicion by the Crown. Many Inquisitors believed that they would jump at the chance to try and sway others over to their old faith."

The guide backed away a few steps from the antechamber, towards the door. Perhaps subconsciously signaling he was ready to go. His eyes looked uneasy as he stared over the edge of the platform, down towards the pit of unfortunate souls.

Bree took his lead. She moved to the exit, glancing once more over her shoulder at the pit of men, women and children who had gone forgotten for centuries.

Suddenly, the loss of her grandmother struck her on the way back up to the cathedral. She followed the diminutive man back through the threshold of the catacombs, back into the cool, crisp air of the basilica, sobs clinging to the back of her throat.

Bree was irritated with herself that now, of all times, she felt the urge to cry. But something about seeing how the world disregarded all of the tortured people reminded her of how forgotten her grandmother had seemed when she went to the nursing home to visit her in her final moments. It hit her with a wave of profound sadness and she suddenly felt incredibly alone.

Over 3,000 miles away from David, her only friend in the world. In a strange country. Just weeks after the death of her beloved grandmother. The last person she considered family. Though her mother still breathed, she felt as if she had died the same night her father did.

She grabbed a crumpled 50 Sol bill from her pocket and pressed it into the gentleman's hand as she walked from the church and onto the front steps. A large gathering of people milled about, lingering on the steps, chatting with each other, tourists taking photos of the Plaza de Armas, a few policia milling around near the Government Palace, black riot shields in front of them, large automatic weapons on their backs.

She turned her face up to the gray sky for just a moment, relieved to feel the first few cool raindrops of a refreshing storm on the horizon. Bree closed her eyes and took a deep breath. When she opened them again, there was a man by her side.

His face was filthy and he wore a stained, tattered pair of khakis. He had on a flannel shirt that looked caked in dirt. The man smiled at her, his teeth yellowed with decay and his brown eyes sparkled.

"I have something you might like," he said to her softly, almost too softly for her to hear.

Bree began to wave him off, but his hand came out of the pocket of his flannel shirt so quickly and she saw what he held.

It was a rosary. Worn down. Very old. All wooden beads, with a small crucifix on one end. All wooden beads except for one stone. Bree was immediately intrigued.

"What is this?" She asked him, her eyes narrowing.

"It is a very old rosary," he whispered, looking over his shoulder at the policia who seemed disinterested. "It is hundreds of years old.

It was recovered from one of the remains in the cathedral."

"Wait a minute. You mean the catacombs? This was found in the catacombs?" Bree asked eagerly.

"Yes," he said, again softly, his eyes darting quickly around him. "Here, take a look."

He handed the rosary to her and she ran the beads through her fingers. She could tell that it was very delicate, very old. Bree was almost afraid to touch it for fear that the thread holding the beads together would break. Her eyes moved to the one strange looking bead. It looked like a milky white stone of some kind, an odd-looking dark shadow hidden within. Her eyes fixated on it, feeling an odd attachment to the rosary, and suddenly she knew that she had to bring it home.

Maybe it was the feeling of immense sadness that she had felt for the forgotten souls in the catacombs, but she felt like bringing home the rosary might somehow make whoever owned it live on.

Indefinitely.

"Cuanto cuesta?" She asked, her eyes not straying far from the beautiful rosary.

"100 Soles," he replied. She handed over the money without another thought to haggle. He grabbed the cash, called out a thanks and was gone.

She stood in the pooling rain, still on the steps of the basilica, her fingers trailing over the rosary curiously. Bree felt a strange surge flow through her, almost fuzzy and thick. It felt as if she was precisely where she was meant to be at precisely the right time.

A grin snaked its way across her lips as she delicately placed the rosary in her pocket and began the long walk back to her hotel.

Bree took a turn on Avenida Garcilaso de la Vega, enjoying the Parque Cahuide on the right, when she stumbled upon a strange yellow house. There was a small gathering of people outside, listening to a Peruvian tour guide as they stood taking pictures.

As she neared the group, she began to hear what the guide was saying.

"...Casa Matusita has a very bad history. It was rumored that one of the first owners of this building was burned alive during the Inquisition."

Bree's attention was piqued and she glanced over at the group, lingering for a moment near a park bench just to hear what else was being said.

"Her name was Parveneh Dervaspa. Back in the mid-1700s, during the tail end of the Inquisition, she was tortured by Inquisitors for being a witch. They claimed that she cured diseases that plagued the capital and they were able to, through torture, get her to confess that her powers came from hell. She was condemned to die at the stake. Legend says that as she was writhing in the fire, she laid a curse on anyone who entered the house.

"Ever since then, horrible things have happened in this house. A couple of specific examples is a tale of a Japanese couple with two children that moved into the home. The husband came home one day and found his wife in bed with another man. In a rage, he murdered them both, then lay in wait for his children to come home to murder them as well. Afterwards, he practiced 'harakiri,' or 'seppuku' on himself, committing suicide by disembowelment.

"Another tale is told of a master who was cruel to his servants. One night, during a party the master held, his servants got revenge by putting a powerful hallucinogen into the food and drinks. And then they waited and listened to the dying cries of the dinner party. When they entered the room, well, let's just say it wasn't the tidiest scene. Mutilated bodies, intestines and blood smeared all over the walls. To say nothing of the several people who have merely wandered into the home throughout the years and disappeared.

"Many people attribute this back to the curse. And blame Parveneh solely for all of the pain and torment that occurred at this house. It was not uncommon for individuals tortured and killed by the Inquisition to vow revenge. There were a number of curses laid bare on Inquisitors back in those days, a number of them that seemed to come to fruition."

At the mention of a curse, Bree froze. The hair on the back of her neck began to bristle. She wasn't quite sure why, but her fingers absentmindedly rubbed against the rosary in her pocket. It felt hot to the touch.

Shaking her head and walking away, she moved quickly, noticing the sun was beginning to set and the early evening had begun to descend. She glanced up at the Casa Matusita for just a brief moment and saw a woman in the window. She was quite beautiful, young, voluptuous, wearing a long gown, her hair wild and dark around her shoulders. She smiled down at Bree, a strange, knowing kind of smile, and no one in the crowd seemed to be looking up at her.

They were all preoccupied with taking pictures of the building, listening to the tour guide drone on about the tormented tales of the building, but no one glanced her way.

A chill ran through Bree's body and she turned away, her feet picking up speed. She wanted to get to her hotel before dark.

She lingered for a moment outside of her hotel, her eyes gazing over to the fluorescent lights of a pub on the ground level.

The walk back to the hotel took longer than she anticipated, and she didn't dare hail a cab with what little Spanish she knew. Lima was the type of city that didn't exactly cater to the foreigners. For being a metropolitan area of South America, there weren't a lot of locals that knew English, she found.

By the time she finally got back to her hotel, feet hurting and exhausted, the darkness of the night had seeped in around her.

Yet the appeal of a drink before going upstairs was strong.

Bree opened the door and wandered into a small dimly lit pub. It was charming but very well appointed; a large mahogany wall behind the bar lit from beneath, bottles and bottles of expensive alcohol appointing it. On the back side there was a large mirror running the length of the bar.

Bree hesitated for a moment, seeing the mirror, remembering…

But the bar was fairly well lit, and she wasn't alone. The bartender was wiping down the far corner of counter and there was a man sitting on the other end.

A fancy looking man. Wearing tails and a top hat.

It struck Bree as incredibly strange; it wasn't something that you saw people wear anymore. It was very old fashioned but in remarkably good condition. Not moth-eaten or worn like she would expect if it spent years in the back of an old closet.

Nonetheless, she spied the whiskey, and her mouth began to water. She moved over to a bar stool next to the man, waved her hand at the bartender and smiled meekly as he walked over.

"Whiskey, please. Johnnie."

The bartender nodded in understanding and went to work pouring a glass.

Bree's eyes moved slowly over the back of the bar but then diverted quickly. She didn't want to look in the mirror. She wanted to avoid it at all costs.

The scarf around her neck was tighter than this morning, and she knew she was still fighting the swelling. Whatever happened to her was true.

It was real.

It was still lingering around her throat.

And she was in no hurry to test her luck to see if the man was still with her.

The man next to her shifted and cleared his throat. A smell

wafted to her nose suddenly, very faint and dim.

She couldn't quite place it...

The bartender put her glass down on the counter and took the soles that she handed him. She quickly brought the glass to her lips, ice cubes striking her teeth, and took a long drink.

The whiskey went to work running slowly down her throat, hot and rich into her belly. It was delicious.

"I know you," the man next to her said.

For a second, it took Bree a moment to register that he had said anything, let alone that he was directing her. He didn't turn in her direction, didn't move an inch. He just sat at the bar, nursing a drink between his fingers, staring ahead.

Bree couldn't see his face, but he sat in front of the long mirror, running the length of the bar.

Bree couldn't bring herself to look.

"Excuse me?" She cleared her throat.

He didn't stir. Just sat there silently, his fingers slowly turning the glass in his hands. The bartender seemed to have disappeared. Either bored or disinterested in the two of them.

After a long moment, he spoke again.

"Oh yes, I know you." His voice was very soft, unsettling. As if he had the confidence of knowledge, of knowing things, of wisdom. It sounded oddly hollow, like there was no depth behind it. No feeling or emotion.

It troubled her.

"I seriously doubt that, sir," she replied, staring down at her drink, counting the ice cubes. She refused to look up and straight ahead, into the mirror. She didn't want to see his face.

The smell was there again, something fiery and burning but still too soft to get an idea of what it was. It seemed to be permeating off of him.

"I've watched you for a while now." He said simply, with no indication of supplying more. His voice had turned gravelly, a bit deeper.

Her blood ran cold. Yet she was stuck to the seat, she couldn't bring herself to move. As if in reply, her throat began to ache, phantom wounds that she was suddenly very aware of. She didn't want another repeat of last night. And yet her limbs would not cooperate with her. They refused to move.

Bree had no choice but to sit and listen to what he had to say.

She had a feeling whatever he was about to say would terrify her.

"You think you're alone, but you were never quite alone." He said, bemused. She couldn't bear to look at his face, either by turning her head slightly or glancing at the mirror.

She was terrified of what she might see. Something about this man was not right.

The smell…

And then it hit her all at once. She knew what the smell was that seemed to permeate and seep from his pores.

Sulfur.

The man smelled of sulfur.

"I'm not sure what you mean," she faltered.

The man started to heave, very slightly, and it took her a moment to realize that he was laughing dryly, deliberately.

"I think you do," he replied.

Another twirl of the glass with his fingers.

Knotted fingers, longer fingernails than necessary, yellowed with age. And the smell of sulfur. And heat. Heat seemed to be rising from his coat, the sleeves of his jacket ill-fitting. Shorter than his arms. With one hand, he pulled his top hat lower onto his brow, shrouding his face from her, even though she wasn't trying to look at it.

The words flew from her mouth before she had time to stop them. She didn't want to ask him, because she knew she'd get the answer.

And she didn't want to hear the answer.

Didn't want it to be said aloud.

Yet the question was out there, hanging in the air, unavoidable.

"What are you?" She asked him, her eyes numbly gazing at the melting ice in the whiskey glass. Her mouth was suddenly dry, parched, but she couldn't bring herself to take a sip. Couldn't bring herself to do anything that might mean accidentally gazing his face in the mirror, accidentally catching a reflection.

Her ears remained peeled, desperate for a sound from the back room, from the bartender who had so studiously disappeared.

Again, another bout of laughter, sardonic and uneasy. Bree noticed how very close his arm was to her, realizing how close she had sat next to him. It was suddenly a very claustrophobic feeling, stifling and unbearable.

"I don't need to say it. You already know." His long-clawed fingers finally picked up the glass he had been twirling and took a nice long drink.

There was an odd sizzling sound as he swallowed, and a metallic smell filled the air. Then it was gone.

"'There is special providence in the fall of a sparrow.'" He said to her softly, his empty glass slowly lowered to the counter.

Bree didn't look up.

"Hamlet." She replied.

"Well done," he retorted. "Now tell me what it means."

Bree tried to move her leg from behind the bar stool, tried to step down, to get away, to move away from this man. This thing.

She had her suspicions about what he was.

But she couldn't bring herself to even think it…

Her body was not cooperating. She wasn't interested in a literary lesson.

"Tell me what it means, Bree," he hissed insidiously.

Of course he knew her name.

"It has to do with fate," she replied begrudgingly.

"And? Go on." He hissed.

She shifted uncomfortably on the stool.

"The inevitability of fate. Hamlet accepted the truth; that there is a guiding force pushing us along a predestined path. That he was powerless. That he had no control."

The man shifted, hissed through his teeth, started to laugh again.

"Do you believe that?" He asked her.

Bree shook her head slowly from side to side, her fingers cold from gripping her glass of whiskey. "What does it matter what I believe?" She asked.

He laughed again, the smell of sulfur now stronger than before.

"I think you'll find that it will. It will matter, Bree."

And then he stood up, turned, and was gone.

Bree sat at the counter for a few minutes more, her fingers and knuckles white against the glass, terrified to look up, to move, to do anything other than wait.

Just then the bartender came around the corner, carrying a heavy crate full of bottles. He put it on the counter and slowly began restocking his bar.

Sensing he was there made Bree feel a bit more at ease. She turned his direction.

"Sir, sir?" She called to the bartender.

He looked her way, exasperated for the interruption when the hour was getting late and he had chores to finish.

"Si, madam?"

"Who... who was that man?"

He looked at her confused, and then shook his head with frustration. He thought she was playing a joke.

"Very funny, madam," and he turned back to his crate, unloading bottles two at a time.

"I'm not trying to be, sir. The gentleman in the top hat. He was hard to miss. He was sitting right next to me, for Christ's sakes!"

She continued, growing scared and angry. This couldn't be happening again.

Was she going mad?

Was she losing her mind?

She finally turned to the side, to show the bartender the empty glass he left behind.

But there was nothing. No remnants at all of anyone having been there.

"Madam, there was no one here but you."

Stunned and terrified, she threw down a tip to the bartender and hurried to her room upstairs.

From her bag she produced her laptop. Logged on.

Changed her return flight departure to a few days earlier.

She was done with Peru.

CHAPTER FOUR
OUIJA

October 1999

The cool autumn wind blew harshly and she pulled her light jacket closer to her. The streetlights had finally popped on and the streets were quiet. Bree knew that her Mom would soon be calling for her to come home, but she didn't care.

There was an urgency in Solveig's voice when she called, insisting that Bree come over immediately. She had to obey.

Her friend's freckled face greeted her at the door before she even had a chance to knock. Her hazel eyes were wild and her skin moist and slick with sweat.

"Sol, what…" Bree began but was pulled inside the house. All of the lights were off except for the dimly lit hall, leading up the curved staircase. Solveig put a finger up to her own lips and looked excitedly down the hall, towards the family room. Bree then heard the small drone of canned laughter, the flickering light of a television being cast into the hallway.

Without a word, Solveig dragged her best friend up the stairs and into her bedroom. Bree laughed when they reached the sanctuary of her room, and slowly started taking off her jacket, glancing around at the familiar boy band posters on the wall that they'd drooled over numerous times before.

"Alright, Sol, you got me here. I might be grounded already.

What was all this about?" Bree asked her friend, her arms crossing in front of her.

Without another word, Solveig flew over to her bed and dropped to her knees, her arms disappearing into the darkness beneath her bed and coming out with a Ouija board.

A dark shadow fell over Bree's face. "You seriously brought me over here for this garbage?"

"Bree, I stole it from my parent's room and wanted to try it out with you. You've just got to try it with me!" She begged, her eyes wide.

"This is trash. You know this isn't even real. I don't want to mess around with this stuff," she said, grabbing her jacket and moving towards the door.

Solveig grabbed her arm roughly. Bree turned back to her and saw something different in her friend's eyes. Something resembling a dark desperation. "Please. Please, Bree. For me."

She was immediately suspicious. "Why do you want this so badly? I've never even heard you utter anything related to wanting to mess with this trash before now. Why, Sol?"

Tears came now, springing up to her friend's eyes and her grip lessened on Bree's arm. She turned away entirely before Bree caught a quick glimpse of what appeared to be shame.

Solveig stood with her back to Bree for a moment before she croaked out, "I just need to. We need to do this."

Bree threw her jacket back on the canopy bed. She sighed.

"Okay, Sol. This obviously means more to you than it does to me.

So, let's do it." She dropped down to the floor in front of the board, staring at it warily for a moment.

Solveig turned back to her, a big, thankful grin on her face. Tears streaked down her ruddy cheeks. She sat down across from her friend on the other side of the board, rolling up her sleeves. As she rolled up her left sleeve, Bree saw bruises on her friend's arm. She started to say something but Solveig noticed her reaction and rolled her sleeve back down quickly, not meeting her eyes.

Bree was a little taken aback by her friend's extreme reactions to wanting to do this. And the relief that she so obviously felt when Bree conceded. It made her a little cautious. But the truth was, she would do anything for Solveig.

"Okay, I think we're both supposed to place our fingers on the pointer like this," Solveig began, putting her index and middle fingers of both hands on either side of the planchette.

Bree mimicked her and stared at her quietly for a moment.

"Now what?"

"Now you ask questions," she said.

"Me? I didn't want to do this in the first place!" Bree said.

Solveig, for a moment a flash of concern passing over her features, recovered quickly and replied, "Okay, I'll start."

Solveig cleared her throat and asked, "Is anyone there?"

They sat in silence for what seemed to be a long while. Bree was growing exasperated; it was past dinnertime, her stomach grumbled angrily in response, and here she was, possibly facing a harsh punishment at home for being late, doing something she never thought she'd ever do.

Then something strange happened.

The hairs on the back of her arms seemed to stand on end; the air took on an almost thick, electric feel. She glanced up at Solveig who seemed just as surprised.

And then the planchette shot over to the word "YES" so quickly they almost lost their grip.

"Sol... did you..."

Solveig just shook her head mutely. Cleared her throat. "I guess we should keep going," she said quietly, very obviously scared.

"I think we should stop this right now," Bree said out loud, dispassionately, almost without feeling of any kind. Part of her was intrigued; she knew that something ethereal had happened, was happening, and her pure, morbid curiosity prevented her from taking her fingers off the planchette, from getting her jacket on, from leaving the room and walking home.

She needed to hear more.

Solveig ignored her superfluous plea. "What is your name?"

Again, they sat there waiting for something to happen. The energy around them in the room seemed to hum, and it both frightened and fascinated Bree at the same time. She knew she should stop at this point, but she just couldn't. It was like she was drawn to this thing, this entity, spirit... whatever it was. She just needed to hear it through.

The planchette slowly started to move again, working its way across the board to the first letter. Bree looked up at Solveig, who refused to meet her gaze. Her eyes were instead focused on the board, eagerly awaiting the name of this thing that they had conjured up.

The first letter was A. It slowly moved to the next. L.

And then it moved to T.

And then E.

Finally, resting on R.

"'Alter?' What kind of name is Alter?" Bree asked, once again looking up at her friend.

Solveig, again, seemed so entranced with the board that she couldn't look away. She was a girl possessed at this point; she had to ask her next question, said with such a hasty desperation that, once again, Bree felt she wasn't getting quite the full story in this entire situation.

"What do you want?"

Again… that half second hesitation that seemed to accompany this stranger. And then the planchette moved to K.

And then I.

Quickly over to L.

And then it did another loop and came back to settle on L again.

Bree took her fingers away from the board. Stood up and grabbed her jacket without another word.

Solveig stared up, tears standing in her eyes, begging to burst forth. "Bree!"

"No, enough! Enough, Sol! This is garbage! I don't know who this Alter is or why he wants to kill, but I've heard enough. I don't ever want to see you again." She said, her words harsh even to her ears. But something stirred within Bree, something delicate within that she suddenly felt very protective of. And whatever binds were broken in just the last five minutes, she had to admit to herself: she was terrified.

She bolted out of the room, leaving Solveig sitting on the floor, tears running down her cheeks. Out the front door and back into the cold night.

The streetlights were fully alight now, washing a dim glow against the silhouettes of cars parked on the side of the road. She threw her jacket on over her shoulders, zipped it up angrily, and held back a sob.

She wasn't sure what had just happened. It all felt a little too much like a strange nightmare that she was having difficulties waking up from. And Solveig was so insistent, suspiciously insistent…

Bree was about a block away from Solveig's house when she heard footsteps. Normally the sound of footsteps behind her wouldn't send a ripple of fear down her spine, but considering what she had just witnessed, it did. Quickly, she turned to look behind her.

The streetlights bathed the pavement in an odd greenish hue, pushing back the deepening black sable of the shadows beyond. A shiver ran across her; it was far too dark. Far too fast.

Amid the deepening shadows, her eyes caught movement. Ever so slight. There was a figure there, a shadow that moved in the darkness beyond, walking slowly down the middle of the street, where the strength of the lights could just barely reach. The figure moved slowly, about 200 feet behind her, not in any real hurry to catch up to her.

Relax, she told herself. *It's probably someone out for a late night walk. Just relax.*

It wasn't until she heard the figure call her name, in an insidious hiss carrying on the breeze, that she froze. Turned back again.

This time, the figure had somehow, inexplicably, gained ground. He was now only about 100 feet away, slowly catching up to her. And she could see him for what he was.

An old man. Clad in a heavy, brown cloak. It looked old, almost otherworldly. Like he didn't quite fit into the landscape of suburban houses and streets and stop signs and cars parked on the sides of the road.

He was ethereal and grotesque; his eyes were beady and almost sunken in and black. Yet she could feel their gaze, very intentional and powerful. His teeth protruded out from his sallow, cracked lips, sharp and oddly misshapen. Gnarled hands bulged out from below the sleeves of his heavy cloak, fingernails long and yellowed.

She could smell him. The scent was overpowering and hit her all at once, with the force of a storm gale. The odor of cat urine was overwhelming... cat urine and decay. Of old things that were meant to be dead, buried, forgotten; not standing in the middle of a darkened street.

"Bree." He stated simply, his voice surprisingly clear.

That was all the encouragement Bree needed. She turned quickly on her heel and began to run, wanting to scream, to make the wildest most impossibly horrid sounds to get attention, to get neighbors to come outside and turn on their porch lights and witness this, to see that she was being chased by something ancient and long dead.

But she couldn't make a sound. The only thing she could hear was the maddening stomp of her feet on the hard pavement, the wheezing sound between her teeth as she pushed herself faster and harder, to get closer to her house.

She could see it just ahead, the simple mailbox with "Ward" emblazoned in block letters on the side. Bree wanted so badly to cry out, call her mother's name, see her flip on the porch light, open the door, alight upon the stoop, widen her arms and catch Bree mid-flight.

Again… her words failed her. The light remained dark. The house beyond silent. The street remained completely empty. Save for the crazed panting of a young girl, terrified beyond belief.

Could this have anything to do with the Ouija board? With what she and Solveig had just done? Is this related at all?

The thoughts were merely just passing fancies in the immediacy of the situation. She was terrified to turn her head, to look behind her, to see this creature somehow ever closer than before, possibly reaching out one of those gnarled hands to her flesh, ready to sink his nails into her skin…

The Zimmerman's house was off to the right, their big bay window in their front room dark, curtains drawn. Yet she could catch her reflection, as she often did when riding her bike down the street in the daylight. She loved to turn her head ever so slightly to the right and see the pink streamers on her handlebars swaying in the wind as she rode past.

By sheer reflex, she passed the house and her head turned slightly right, her eyes gazing at the darkened glass, catching her reflection in the glass. Her eyes crazed, her legs pumping as she ran as fast as she could down the road.

But she saw something else too. Something terrifying.

As her feet pounded the pavement, her lungs feeling like they were ripping open and spilling into her chest... she saw something else. And it wasn't quite what she expected.

She expected to see the figure behind her, chasing after her. Possibly reaching out to her with those awfully horrid gnarled hands.

What she saw instead forced her to regain her voice. Her breath, what little was left in her lungs, burst forth and she let out a loud, terrifying scream that echoed through the darkened streets.

There, hunched on her shoulders, crouched down and clinging to her back, was the man. His head turned to the glass as she passed the window and he smiled.

Her screams finally let out, she saw the light turn on, the door open, and her mother was suddenly there, staring in incredulity at her daughter, running and sobbing and screaming towards her.

She flew to her mother, wrapped her arms around her and pushed her inside the house, slamming the door shut with a backwards kick.

"Bree! What in the..."

She turned and saw her reflection again in the mirror next to the side table in the foyer. It was just her, being embraced by her mother, her eyes wide with horror.

"Bree, what's going on? Are you okay? Where have you been? What the hell happened?" She tried to pull away from her daughter to get a better look at Bree's face, but Bree held her tightly.

That was when there was a knock on the door.

Frozen solid, Bree again stared at their reflection in the mirror. Her mother made a move to the door, but Bree stopped her.

"No, please, please don't!" She begged, her eyes wide and terrified and staring at the door.

"For God's sakes, Bree, you need to get a grip," her mother said, staring at her daughter with an equal mix of curiosity and exasperation.

She went over to the door as Bree backed away, sinking slowly against the wall. Though she wanted to move, wanted to run away again, she couldn't. Whatever morbid curiosity made her stay to finish the Ouija board with Solveig was the same power that kept her feet planted firmly where they were, waiting to see exactly what lay behind the door.

Her mother gripped the doorknob. Gave one last quick, confused glance over her shoulder towards her daughter and opened the door.

Standing on the stoop, bathed awash in the brutally potent light of the porch, was the man. Smiling that horridly twisted smile, one of his gnarled hands slowly rising up, pointing at her. He didn't say a word, but just stood there and stared at her, almost bemused and humored.

Bree's knees knocked, and her bladder released. She could feel the warm stream of urine running down her legs as her eyes filled with fresh tears, eager sobs ready to break away from her throat.

Her mother turned back to Bree, seeing her terror and fright, staring at the open maw of the door, and asked, "What is it, Bree? There's nothing there."

It hit her then, with an alarm ringing hollowly and loudly in her brain... that her mother couldn't see this creature.

"He...he's right there, Mom." She croaked out, her throat pained and sore and raw as she pointed at him. Bree raised her eyes again to the stoop... and he was gone.

Disappeared.

Her mother hadn't seen him. Couldn't see him. Bree didn't know whether that made her relieved or even more alarmed. If she could see this monster and her mother couldn't, was she going mad?

And then a name came to the forefront of her mind, and she couldn't stop herself from uttering it aloud: "Alter."

Her mother shut the door, moving towards her. "Alter? What does that mean?"

Bree shook her head quickly, side to side, as if to shake all that had transpired that evening from her mind. She began to sob and just wanted to be held by her mother, absorbed by her familiar arms.

Her mind couldn't process what had just happened.

She let her mother hold her and she just prayed.

She prayed that nothing like this would ever happen to her again.

She prayed that her life would only be happiness and joy moving forward.

She prayed that she would never see Alter again.

…

She was wrong on all counts…

CHAPTER FIVE
HEREDITARY

She unlocked the front door and entered the dark corridor, throwing the keys down on a nearby side table. Bree reached over and turned on a small lamp, bathing the living room in an eerie glow.

Boxes were still stacked up around her, remnants and reminders that her grandma was gone and there was still much to do. For a moment she berated herself for not taking care of everything before she left. But she remembered how overwhelming it was when she left, in addition to the interest from the media about her involvement with Randall Carlisle. When she flew into the JFK airport, the throng of reporters had dwindled or lost interest entirely. They had moved onto other stories, sinking their teeth into someone else's flesh.

Aside from the rosary, Bree didn't feel like she came back with much, other than some sad stories of the history of the place.

Bree grabbed her phone and shot a quick text message to David. He replied back quickly and told her he was on his way over.

She knelt down in front of one of the many boxes Grandma Doris kept in the attic. Taking a deep breath, she reached in and grabbed out an old shoebox. It was covered in a thick layer of dust. She wiped it off with her sleeve and opened the lid.

Inside, there was only one object. Her eyes narrowed in confusion. Why would Grandma Doris have kept a scrapbook in a shoebox in the attic? Wouldn't this have been something that she would have wanted to keep within reach?

Bree opened up the old book and was surprised to see the disarray. Usually her grandmother was very neat and organized. However, inside the scrapbook there were a number of random newspaper articles, photos, and computer printouts on strange things.

Suddenly very intrigued, Bree laid the book on the floor in front of her and pulled every loose-leaf paper from its pages. She lined each piece up in front of her and stared for the longest time at the assortment of random papers.

Nothing seemed to be connected. Usually most scrapbooks have family pictures, organized by time, organized by event, organized by some sort of method.

But there was no rhyme or reason as to why Grandma Doris kept these things in one place.

There were post-it notes, loose leaf lined paper with things and names scribbled on them, even what looked like a family tree.

Bree picked up the family tree that was very crudely drawn. The page had started to yellow with age, but she recognized Grandma Doris' handwriting. The lineage went back to the 1500s.

Bree was impressed; she never knew her grandma was into genealogy. She had obviously done a fair share of research into their family tree to find all the info.

Her eyes trailed the tree back and back and back… to the first person on the list. The name Francesco jumped out at her, born 1578. But there was a crudely scrawled word next to it in her grandma's handwriting that she could barely make out.

Bree brought the paper closer to her face, squinting her eyes and her blood ran cold.

The word was, "Cursed."

"Cursed, Gram?" Bree asked out loud to the empty house. "What does that mean?"

Immediately her thoughts wandered back to the tour guide lingering in front of Casa Matusita, and the horrid story he told about the curses from the Inquisition.

There was a loud knock on the door and Bree jumped.

Turned.

David came in, a broad smile on his face. "B! You're back!" He ran to her and hugged her before she could slow her racing heart.

Immediately he could tell there was something wrong.

"What happened?" He asked, his once smiling eyes now drawn in concern for his friend.

Bree shook her head hastily side to side, as if to banish the thoughts. "Nothing. I'm fine. God, it's good to see you, Davey." She replied, smiling up at him.

He joined her on the floor where she sat cross-legged and gave a cursory glance to the documents spread before her.

"I hate to ask," David laughed as he ran his fingers through his hair and shot her a smile.

"I'm just finally getting around to going through some of her things. It hasn't been easy," Bree replied.

"I know, B." She felt his hand hover on her back for a moment and then it was gone. He looked over at her, his eyes narrowing suspiciously for a moment.

"What the hell is that?" He asked, pointing to her neck.

Bree's heart did a little jump, suddenly realizing that she forgot to put a scarf on, and she self-consciously adjusted her shirt collar.

"It's nothing."

"The fuck it is, Bree! What the hell happened?" He was growing angry with her, frustrated that she wasn't being honest with him.

She just shook her head in silence, trying to focus instead on the papers in front of her.

David, in an uncharacteristic move, knocked the papers out of her hand. He grabbed her hands in his, forced her to turn to him.

"Alright, enough of this garbage now, understand? Enough! You are going to tell me what the hell is going on. Right now. Do you understand?" His words were sharp, pointed. But his eyes were warm, concerned.

Genuine.

Bree nodded silently. Her voice wavered as she began to tell him everything. About the Ouija board she played with as a little girl, the man she saw, the man who stalked her in the shadows of her youth, that no one else seemed to be able to see, the man who choked her in her hotel bathroom in Peru. The man she was terrified would one day murder her.

She told him about the strange woman no one seemed to be able to see in the Casa Matusita. About the strange man at the bar.

She told him about the night her father was killed. About her mother, about Solveig, she came clean about everything. She spared herself nothing. Bree knew that David would likely think she was insane. But it felt good to talk about it, to finally get it off her chest. To bring the darkness to the light. It somehow seemed to take the power away.

When she was done, David sat in silence, absorbing all that he had just heard. Bree chewed her lip nervously, worried that he might get up and walk out, and then she would lose the last person that she truly had.

But he didn't move. He just sat on the floor, staring at her thoughtfully. After a moment, he turned and looked at the papers strewn before her. And saw the word "Cursed" scribbled hastily next to the first name on her family tree.

"Does that say 'Cursed?'" He asked her. She sighed deeply, relieved, realizing that he wasn't going to be frightened away so easily.

"I think it does." She flipped through some of the loose pieces of paper.

"I don't know why I'm getting this feeling that this all has something to do with my family," she said to David.

It was quiet for a moment in the room.

There. She had said it. The suspicion that she so carefully guarded nearest to her heart, the thing that she was most terrified to state aloud to anyone, she finally said it.

She had a feeling that all of this awful stuff that had been happening to her had something to do with her family.

"When I was in Peru, I passed by a tour guide who was talking about curses. And then coming back here and seeing this scribbled on my family tree. It can't be a coincidence. It's too eerie to be a coincidence." She said.

David chewed on it silently for a minute, picking up the family tree himself and looking over it carefully. After a moment of study, he pulled the paper closer to his eyes and squinted hard.

"What the hell is this?"

"What?"

"This branch of the tree right here, right off of your Grandma Doris' line." He pointed it out to her.

There was the line denoting her father, dearly departed, and the marriage to her mother. Below it was her name. But there was another line, another child, offshooting from her grandparents and away from the rest of the tree.

David looked puzzled. "Does this mean…"

"I have no idea. But," she sighed deeply. "But I think I know someone who might."

The hallway was lined with pea green lineoleum and smelled like disinfectant. Deep within the bowels of the building she could hear a woman screaming bloody murder. There were rows of padded benches lining the walls of the corridor, a handful of people littering them. One woman rocked back and forth, mumbling incoherently to herself as they walked past.

Bree's heart wrenched in her chest. She was here to see her mother, who she hadn't seen for almost two decades. Bree harbored a lot of anger and resentment towards her, a woman who had once been very kind and loving. For the brief time in her youth that she could remember.

Before Randall Carlisle.

Before that night.

Since then, Gina Ward had become an embarrassment to her daughter, someone she would rather pretend no longer existed. For the first ten years, Bree felt terribly guilty for feeling that way. But then she spent the next ten realizing that her mother likely didn't even know who she was.

This brought on a fair mix of relief and sadness. She loved her mother, who her mother had once been anyway, but she just chose to no longer have her in her life. It was as simple as that.

Again, part of the element around changing her last name, to escape that moment. That period of her life. To break free from those binds.

Visiting her mother on a regular basis in a place like this would only drive back home the horrible certainty that her father was dead.

That she was alone.

It was something she'd rather avoid.

The nurse's station loomed ahead. Without a glance, Bree reached out for David's hand. He gripped it tightly in his own as they approached the nurse.

"Hi, I'm here to visit a patient," Bree started.

"Name?"

"Um… Breanna Ward."

The nurse looked confused for a moment and then laughed.

"No, dear, I mean the name of the patient."

Bree sighed. "Oh, I'm sorry. Um, Gina Ward."

The nurse scribbled something on a clipboard and had them sign their names. She printed out two badges that said "Visitor" and told them that they could find her in the west wing.

Bree and David started for the west wing, his hand still clasping hers tightly. Her stomach did a flip.

"I don't know if I can do this," she said nervously. "I haven't seen her for almost twenty years, Davey. What do I even say to her? This could be a total waste of our time. She probably doesn't even remember me, let alone remember anything from the past."

"Don't start talking that way," David said. "You're defeating yourself before you've even started. Let's just give it a try. Like you said, you feel like there's something we're missing here. She could be the key to us figuring this out."

They walked down the hallway into an alcove that had WEST WING emblazoned on it. Inside there was a large activities room littered with tables. Strewn on the tables were a variety of puzzles and games with about a dozen women milling around.

There was a couch in a far corner, a large old-fashioned console television blaring in the background. Nobody appeared to be watching it.

Bree stopped and stood, staring at each of the women in the

room, wondering if she would recognize her when she saw her.

Her eyes scoured the room, looking for someone that held some semblance of the woman that she used to know.

Her eyes stopped; her blood froze.

"Davey," she started.

"Did you find her?" He asked, entirely unhelpful as he didn't know what her mother looked like. David followed her gaze.

There was a girl hunched over in a chair. Her red hair was messed up and she was muttering to herself softly, but Breanna was positive that it was Solveig.

"That can't be your mother," David said.

"No. Not my mother. Someone else I used to know," she replied, already moving over in her direction.

As she walked over there, she replayed the last moments she'd seen Solveig in her mind. Over and over again, she remembered that night. She remembered running from her house after they played with the Ouija board. She remembered screaming she never wanted to see her again.

And she hadn't. Solveig never returned to school after that. Despite Bree's attempts at getting some information from schoolmates and her parents, she never found out what became of her friend. She rode her bike by her house out of sheer curiosity one day and saw a For Sale sign on the front lawn.

As she saw the woman twist and toss her hair back, freckles sprinkling the bridge of her nose, Bree was positive.

This was her old friend.

"Sol?" She called out, and immediately the woman froze. Looked up.

"Who are you?" She asked suspiciously, her eyes inquisitive and darting between Bree and David.

Breanna let go of David's hand and kneeled down in front of her old friend. "Solveig, it's Bree. Do you remember me?"

Solveig stared at her for the longest moment, silent and introspective. Bree could almost see behind the foggy cloud of medication that shrouded her eyes; she could see a spark of recognition.

"Bree?" She finally croaked out, her face crumpling in an expression of despair. "Is that really you?"

Bree started to cry in spite of herself. She brushed a loose strand of hair back from her friend's face and tucked it behind her ear.

"Yes, it's really me. What are you doing here, Sol?"

"Punishment. P-p-p-punishment, punishment," she started muttering, over and over again, stuttering and began rolling her head back and forth, almost like she was chanting.

"Punishment for what, Sol?" Bree put her hands on her friends shoulders, trying to stop her from swaying. "Punishment for what, sweetie?"

Solveig started to laugh, cackling, a loud, dry humor cracked from her mouth. Her eyes flashed wildly and Bree was, for the first time since she started talking to her, suddenly a little frightened. There was something in Solveig right now that she didn't like.

"You know what," she replied matter-of-factly, breaking out into another fit of laughter.

Bree looked up at David and then returned her focus to her friend, gently touching her knee.

"No, I don't know, Sol. Explain it to me."

Solveig stopped laughing and looked at her inquisitively. Almost as if Bree was the stupid one.

"The man. I dreamed about him. He made me do it." Her voice was suddenly very clear and frank, almost like she was herself again for half a second.

This time Bree gripped her shoulders, tightly.

"What man, Sol? What man? What did he make you do?"

David was becoming uneasy. He glanced around warily towards the nurse's station. The brunette nurse was watching them from the corner of the room.

"Bree, she's all drugged up. She doesn't know what she's saying," he said, touching Bree on the back to ease her away.

Bree was unmoving.

"What man, Sol? You have to tell me! Please! What did he make you do?"

For a moment it looked like Solveig was going to break out into another laughing fit, another bit of hysteria. But instead her face crumpled and she began to cry. Softly, tears streaming down her freckled face.

"Every night, Bree, he came to me. Hurt me. Bruised me. Told me about the board. Told me to invite you over. He made me do it, Bree. He wanted me to do it." Sol collapsed in her chair, exhausted.

The nurse was suddenly at their side.

"I'm sorry, but you're going to need to leave," she said, ushering them away. "You're upsetting our patients."

"Solveig. Who is Alter?" Bree asked.

With the mention of his name, her tears came harder. The nurse, upset and angry, ushered them out of the activity room and back towards the entrance.

Bree resisted the nurse.

"I'm sorry, please. I can't leave yet. I haven't seen my mother. Please."

"I really can't have more of that happen," the nurse said.

"I came all this way to see my mother. I haven't seen her in almost twenty years. Please. It's a matter of life and death," Bree pleaded, her eyes big.

The nurse shifted uncomfortably on her feet. "I suppose but please, no more dramatics, okay?"

Bree nodded silently as the nurse went back to her station to hand out medication and make her rounds.

David moved close to her, holding her hands in his own. Quietly he whispered, "Breanna, what was that about?"

"I... I don't even know. I... I remember bruises on Sol's arm the night that we..." Bree shook her head, trying to make sense out of everything she had just learned.

"Alter." She whispered to herself more than to David.

"What?"

"That was his name. The man. The man we contacted that

night. He's the one that I've been seeing. The one that tried to choke me. God, I sound absolutely insane, don't I?"

"Probably not the best place to say something like that," David said, looking around.

"Shit, sorry," her fingers were in her pocket again, caressing the rosary.

She forgot she even had it with her. Without another thought, she pulled it out of her pocket and stared dumbly at it.

"What's that?" David asked.

"It's just a souvenir I picked up from Peru." She ran it through her fingers, slowly eyeing every inch of it. The beads shifted slightly on the aged string, the one randomly bright stone cool while the others were warm.

"Can I see it?" David asked suspiciously, his eyes narrowed on the rosary.

"Sure," Bree replied and went to hand it to him. However, her fingers stayed tightly clenched to one end of the rosary. She couldn't hand it over.

"Bree," David said, grabbing her fingers and forcing them apart. He held it up to the light, twirling it around in his hands, running each bead through his fingers.

He stopped when he came to the crucifix. His eyes grew wide with horror as he wet his thumb with his mouth and wiped something from the back of the cross.

"Um... Bree?"

"Yes."

"I... uh... oh fuck..." His eyes were wide, his face had drained of color. He was as white as a sheet.

"What? What's wrong?"

She quickly snatched the rosary back, turned the crucifix around, looked at the back.

There, emblazoned underneath decades of piled up dirt, was a name. Engraved on the back, marking the true owner of the rosary:

ALTER.

CHAPTER SIX
ASYLUM

"Are you ready to go back in?" David asked her. They were sitting outside in the cool air outside of the sanitarium. Bree needed to catch her breath. She still held the rosary in her hand, staring at it, disbelieving.

"I... I don't understand. What does this mean? How is this even possible?" She stuttered.

David sat down next to her on the bench. His breath puffed out in front of him in plumes in the cool air. "I have no idea. But I don't like it. Whatever it is, this guy or thing, is attached to you somehow. I feel like we're so close to figuring this out. But we need to see your mother."

"I know. I know," she replied. She stood up and turned. "I guess we'd better get this over with. There will be time enough to digest everything."

They went back into the building, back into the activities room. Solveig was gone. Bree felt a little relieved.

Her eyes scoured the room once more, trying to find someone that looked like her mother.

In the farthest corner of the room, sitting in a high back chair, calmly staring out the dirty window was a woman. Her hair was streaked with bits of gray, her face weathered and worn down with stress. But there was something about the way she rested her chin in her hand as her eyes took in the sights of a drawing storm beyond the window.

Something about the way she rested her chin…

Suddenly, Bree's knees felt weak, wobbly. All at once, she was hit with a flood of memories so thick that she lost her breath.

A lot of really amazing memories, Christmas mornings spent gathered around the tree, piles of crumpled foil wrapping paper strewn about, an obnoxious pile of toys at her feet, her mother relaxing in repose on her sofa, her chin resting just so in her hand…

David caught her elbow when he felt her buckle. "Bree, is that her?"

Hot tears sprang to her eyes, stinging them. She could only nod.

This was going to be harder than she thought.

David's grip on her arm tightened. "We don't have to do this. We can just walk away, Bree. You know that we don't have to do this."

Bree shook her head stubbornly, remembering the figure in the mirror, the hands around her throat. She knew that the answer to what was happening to her rested with her mother. She had to know some answers to the burning questions that she had.

Bree took a deep breath, counted to ten, and composed herself. She told herself the hardest part of this entire exercise was to walk over to her mother. With that in mind, she forced her feet to start to move, one in front of the other; she'd convinced herself that she would know exactly what to say by the time she got there.

By the time she finally got there though, standing next to her mother's chair, hovering for a moment, a deep panic set in. Gina slowly turned her head towards her, drinking her in silently with her eyes.

No one spoke. Bree was searching her mother's cerulean eyes for a hint of recognition, a spark of some kind of memory. The last time she had seen her daughter was a long time ago, when she was still an awkward little girl, but Bree had always wondered if there would be a moment like this where she stood in front of her mother, curious and dying to know if she would be recognized.

If Gina recognized her daughter, she made no indication. Her eyes were clouded over with the same fogginess that accompanied everyone languishing in the ward, well fed on medication and complacency.

Unsure of how to feel, Bree sat down in the chair across from her mother, David hovering a fair distance behind them. He wanted to give Bree her privacy. She was thankful for that.

"Gina," Bree began softly.

At the sound of her name, her mother tilted her head softly in Bree's direction.

"Do you know who I am?" She asked her mother.

Gina stared at Bree thoughtfully for a long minute, shaking her head slowly, her eyes still thick in that fog. The delirium that made Bree sad for her mother.

"My name is Breanna," she said, hoping that the sound of her own name might trigger some sort of reaction, some sort of semblance of remembrance.

Again, if it did, Gina was not letting it show.

She nodded silently, waiting for Bree to continue.

Bree sighed deeply, cleared her throat.

"I'm your daughter, Mom."

Gina's eyes narrowed for a moment, finally clearing a bit and studying her a bit more carefully.

Her cracked lips slowly parted, her eyes seemed to fill with tears almost immediately.

"Bree?" She asked, her voice abnormally small.

Bree smiled, tears streaming down her cheeks and she grabbed her mother's cold hand. "Yes, Mom. It's Bree."

Gina smiled then, and it was as if the last twenty years were lifted from her face. Her eyes lit up, brightened her entire smile, her whole face illuminated. She reached out and caressed Bree's cheek with her small, cold hand.

"My Bree. How beautiful you are," she sighed, her tears spilling over unabashedly onto her cheeks.

And all at once, Bree felt a tremendous wave of shame. All this time she had let her mother sit here, fester here, rot here. All because she was terrified of facing the horrible truths that she had ironically already been facing every single day. To think that she could somehow avoid it, change it, do anything other than face it and accept it suddenly seemed incredibly naïve.

And all the time that she had lost with her mother.

She felt deep shame.

"I'm so sorry, Mom," Bree pleaded, pressing her mother's hand against her cheek, tilting her face to feel her. "I should have been here. I should have come to you. I shouldn't have left you here."

Gina sobbed quietly, her eyes full of forgiveness.

The kind of forgiveness only a mother could give.

"Shhh… what's done is in the past. You're here now, Bree. You're here now."

She could sense David shifting uncomfortably behind her and she knew what he was thinking. If only Gina knew why they were truly there; what they really wanted to ask her.

Again, another wave of shame hit as she pressed her mother's hand and spoke again.

"Mom, we've come to ask you some questions," Bree began. With the mention of "we," Gina finally looked behind Bree and saw David hovering.

"This is Davey, Mom. He's my friend." She reached out and pulled David closer to them. He perched himself on the windowsill and crossed his arms across his chest.

Gina studied him for a moment, initially suspicious. Suddenly she softened and smiled at her daughter. "Just a friend?"

Bree blushed, her cheeks blazing red.

"Yes, Mom."

Another uncomfortable shift from David in the corner.

"Listen, Mom. I have some questions for you. And they may seem strange."

Gina's face suddenly darkened. It was as if a shadow had passed over her features and she looked away. She pulled away and sat back in her chair.

"No." She simply replied.

"Please, Mom. It's very important. I need to know more about…" She stopped for a moment. Reached back out for her mother's hand. Grabbed it and held it for a moment before she continued.

"This isn't going to be easy, Mom. It won't be pleasant. But I need you to trust me. And I need you to stay as calm as you possibly can," Bree said, her eyes quickly flitting over to the nurse's station.

"Do you understand, Mom?"

Gina just stared at her silently. She looked like she was trying to figure out where this was leading before Bree had a chance to say it out loud.

"I need you to show me that you understand what I just said to you. This topic is going to upset you. I need you to be prepared for that."

Gina nodded slowly, solemnly, her eyes still a bit confused.

Bree sighed softly.

"I need to talk about Dad."

For a moment, Gina's hand jerked while it was clasped between Bree's own. But then her mother stared at her, almost thoughtfully.

"Your father. What about your father?" She asked, her head tilting to the side thoughtfully.

"I need to talk about the night that he died."

Gina's head suddenly started to shake. She closed her eyes, as if she was trying to shake away the memories that were suddenly flooding her. Bree held steadfast to her hand.

"Mom, remember what I told you. That this wouldn't be an easy topic for you to talk about. But it's been twenty years. I need to ask you some questions. It's time, Mom. It's time to talk about that night. To put it all to rest. I need to know everything you know."

Another tear escaped Gina's eye and stranded itself halfway down her cheek. Her head shook back and forth, back and forth.

"No. Bree, you need to let it lie. You need to bury it in the past. Forget about it. Move on. Live your life. Continue on."

Bree squeezed her mother's hand. Caught her gaze.

"I can't."

Those two words seemed to change Gina's demeanor in a very odd way. The sadness and despair in her eyes were suddenly replaced by something far more potent, far more powerful.

It took Bree half a second to realize what it was.

Fear.

"It's him." Gina said softly, her eyes no longer focused on her daughter, but rather over her shoulder, behind Bree, through Bree. Without moving her gaze from the empty space behind Bree, Gina's fingers traced the remnants of the crude upside-down crucifix that she had carved into her forearm. Bree cringed for a moment, and then realized she was wearing long sleeves; that her mother hadn't seen her scar.

Yet, how did she know it was there?

"Him?" Bree asked, her senses suddenly heightened as well. "Who is he, Mom?"

Gina smiled, eerie and final. It was as if she knew this moment would come. That her entire life was just a precursor to this snapshot in time.

Her eyes moved once more to her daughter's face, a smug, strange smile curling her lips.

"He's evil," she replied simply.

A chill ran through the marrow of her bones.

"Who is he, Mom? What does he want?"

Another giggle. Now it sounded menacing. Maniacal.

Bree prodded again, growing impatient.

"What does he *want?*!"

Gina tilted her head again, a simple expression on her face, as if her daughter was daft for not having figured it out already.

"He wants you."

Another chill ran through Bree's body. She let go of her mother's hand and sat back in the highback chair. David shifted next to her and knelt down at her side.

Her mother was telling her nothing that she didn't already know. And yet hearing her say the words, so matter-of-factly, drove home the simple fact that everything she had believed was true.

This man, this thing, this beast was thirsty for her blood.

And she didn't know why.

Bree leaned forward again, determined.

"What does this have to do with what happened to Dad? What Randall did to him the night that he died?"

Gina sat back, now having gone completely innocently mad. Her face was no longer the visage that had brightened up just a few moments ago.

Now it was a mask of feigned innocence, of fogged stupor.

She stared at her daughter as if she was the mad one.

"Randall." She shook her head simply, giggling softly to herself.

"Randall didn't kill your father, Bree."

Bree blinked.

Once.

Twice.

She couldn't believe what she heard.

"Mom, I was there that night. I saw him with the knife in his hand. I saw him coming down the stairs. I saw him…"

…black eyes, he had black eyes…

"…staring straight at me, Mom. His hands were covered in Dad's blood. Randall Carlisle killed my father."

Gina rocked back in her chair, threw her head up towards the roof and laughed. The laughter peeled from her mouth loud and clear and absolutely insane.

The brunette nurse at the station stirred. Stood up, looked over at them.

Bree wanted to get up and shake her mother.

Violently.

She wanted her to stop with the incessant laughter.

"Randall killed my father!" She continued, throwing it at her louder in order to be heard over the din of her raucous fit.

Gina didn't stop. Her laughs echoed off the walls of the room and Bree could sense the nurse making her way over to them. She knew she didn't have much time.

"Alright, alright, if it wasn't Randall, then who was it?" She cried out, already inherently knowing the answer before her mother could respond.

More laughter. More footsteps from the nurse's station.

Bree stood, leaned forward, screamed in her face.

"Who was it?!"

Suddenly, Gina's demeanor changed again. Her face contorted to one of furious anger, rage. It took Bree aback how unexpectedly it came on.

"He lives on, Bree! He lives on in the Ninth Stone. And you did it! You released him! You didn't think I knew about that, did you? You didn't think I knew about Solveig. You didn't think I knew about the Ouija board. But I saw that thing on your back the night you came home. I see him still, crawling and clinging to you like a bad cyst. He's festering and rotten and ancient and diabolical and he's clinging to you like you're all he wants in this world. And it's all your fault. You've unleashed the demon, the dybbuk! Your uncle Randall didn't change a thing about the curse, he thought he could kill off the family line and that would be the last of us. All because of you. All because of you. You did this! YOU DID THIS!!!"

Her mother's eyes had gone dark, no longer the cerulean blue that she recognized. Almost black. Spittle flew out into Bree's face as she spewed the hateful words towards her daughter and Bree's eyes grew wide in terror.

She fell back just before Gina reached out to grab her. The nurse was there then, grabbing Gina's hands and pulling them behind her back. Gina writhed in anger and let out a screech so loud the other residents stopped to look at what was happening. Her cry was ethereal, otherworldly. Even the nurse seemed surprised.

Without another word, Bree stumbled out of the chair and away, down the hall, out of the wing, bolted from the front door. She stumbled for a moment and fell.

David was there to catch her. He led her over to the same bench they had been on just a while before.

But, oh, the things that had changed since then...

"Did... did you hear what she said, Davey?" Bree asked, her voice meek and small. She hated the way she sounded right now. But her heart was pounding, her pulse racing.

She had to breathe.

David sensed it too.

"We can talk about that in a minute, Bree. But right now you need to relax. Take a couple of deep breaths," he said. Bree looked up at his face for half a second and saw the alarm, the shock, the awe that outlined the lines of his face.

He paced back and forth for a few moments, running his hands through his thick hair, obviously trying to compose himself as well.

There was a commotion from inside the building, screaming and wild laughter. David moved over to Bree and helped her stand.

"We should get out of here."

Twenty minutes later, they were parked in David's Jeep at a

nearby park. The first layer of rainfall had begun and pelted the windows of the Jeep, the wipers working quickly and squeaking in unison.

They were quiet. Absorbing what had just happened.

David was the first to speak.

"Okay, we need to talk about this. There were a lot of things she said that we need to talk about. First of all, the ninth stone?" He looked at her quizzically.

...she understood obsession...

Bree shook her head slowly and said, "I didn't tell you about that because it seemed like such an odd, innocuous thing. Such a minute detail it wasn't worth bringing up. But the... the night that my dad died, my Mom was rocking in the corner talking about a ninth stone. I didn't know what it meant and honestly I still don't. I thought it was just jibberish. The ramblings of a mad woman. But a small part of me began to obsess about it. Crave knowledge about it. I researched it every which way you can possibly think of, trying to uncover some small clue as to what it meant. Thinking that it might somehow explain... explain why my Dad had to die."

Her eyes shifted downward, tears once again stinging them. She shook her head back and forth, trying to make sense of everything she had just learned.

"But I still don't know how she knew about the Ouija board. About Solveig. Unless Sol got caught by her parents and blabbed. But.. Davey... what she said about the thing on my back..."

She felt David's hand on her now, reassuring. Or attempting to.

"Hey, don't think about that, okay? I mean, let's really assess a few things here. Your mom is in a looney bin first off. Sorry, but it's true. She's not the most reliable source of information in the first place. Secondly, whatever that was in there… that didn't seem like your Mom. It was… It was like she changed."

"You saw that too?" Bree asked, her eyes pleading up at David.

He only nodded, realizing that his attempts at calming her down were failing miserably. But he didn't want to admit to himself that he was scared.

Terrified, actually.

"A curse. She said something about a curse. And that family tree Grandma Doris had. That guy, Francisco. Scribbled next to it was 'Cursed.' Do you think that my family is cursed by something? Someone, Davey?"

David sighed. Rubbed the bridge of his nose and looked out the windshield to the rain beyond.

"I guess that all depends on whether you believe it to be true. If you think back on all of the atrocities of the world, all of the deeply held religions and some of the terrible things that happened in the name of religion… These things only held power if you believed in them." He turned to her, his eyes gazing on her face.

"Do… do you believe in fate, Davey?" She asked him, echoing an earlier conversation that she had started to have with him. What felt like a million years ago.

He sighed deeply and ruminated for a moment.

"I don't know. Again, when we're talking about things having their power taken away, it would seem awfully powerless to believe that we're all coasting around on some predestined path. And that absolutely nothing we say or do can change where we ultimately end up. What is the point of that? What lessons are to be learned, Bree?"

She nodded silently for a moment, turned her head away, a tear running down her cheek. Her eyes caught her reflection in the Jeep's side mirror and she started to sob openly.

Ripe, piercing cries peeled from her throat. It seemed very sudden and David was a little surprised. Her eyes widened in fear.

"Davey?"

"Yes, Bree?"

"I believe in fate. I believe that it's inescapable. Unavoidable. I believe it's naïve to think that we have power over anything in this world." Her eyes, wide and frozen in fear, kept focused on the side mirror of the Jeep.

Terrified.

"I also think we need to go back to my Grandma's house, Davey. The last thing my mother said was 'uncle.' She said, 'Uncle Randall.' That family tree, with the mysterious offshoot that we couldn't connect…"

"Oh, sweet Jesus…" David murmured, the tumblers slowly clicking into place. "Oh, my God."

"We need to be sure," Bree said again, the sobs still raging in her throat, her eyes still frozen to the mirror, to her reflection.

David threw the Jeep into gear. Peeled out of the parking lot quickly in the fresh rain as they raced off to her grandmother's house.

The entire time Bree sat, transfixed, eerily so, to the terrifying side mirror of the Jeep.

To her reflection.

To the smiling, ghastly ghoul sitting in the seat behind her...

CHAPTER SEVEN
ALTER

The house was dark, the air stale, when they walked in. Bree ran through quickly, turning on every light she came across. David did the same, remembering what she told him had happened in Peru.

Once the house was ablaze, Bree stood dumbly in the middle of the room, staring emptily at all of the boxes that were still stuffed in every nook and cranny of her grandmother's house.

"Well, first thing's first," David began, pulling out the scrapbook with all of the random bits of paper. They studied the family tree first and saw that there was another line leading from her grandmother and grandfather. Another child.

No name.

A mystery.

Bree's eyes drifted to the seemingly random computer printouts. Useless old online encyclopedia printouts that her grandmother had made about random subjects.

Or so they had seemed at the time.

Bree's blood ran cold when her eyes drifted over one of the pages.

It was a printout about a dybbuk.

"Davey, come here. Didn't my Mom mention something about a demon or a dybbuk?"

He nodded slowly, glancing over her shoulder at the page she held in her trembling hand. He started to read it aloud for her when she couldn't speak.

"'A dybbuk is a malicious spirit hailing from Jewish mythology. It is believed to be the spirit or dislocated soul of a dead person. The name literally translates from Yiddish to adhere or cling.'"

His eyes shot to her, slowly trailing over her back.

He continued to read.

"'Dybbuks usually begin by possessing inanimate objects, such as boxes or possible religious symbols. Much the same as demonic possession, a dybbuk possession stages are similar. Once a dybbuk has been called upon, the transformation begins. The first stage of possession are manifestation and infestation. This is where the host, through the use of a Ouija board or through a surreptitious object, calls upon the dybbuk, almost giving the being permission to take over.'"

"Oh, my God," Bree murmured softly to herself, her hands beginning to shake.

David read on.

"'The second stage is oppression. This is where the dybbuk will try to break the will to live of the target, often ending in violent attacks, bites, scratches, assaults, violence, sleep deprivation. Depression is prevalent in this stage.'"

Bree remained silent.

"'And the third and final stage: full possession. When the spirit takes over completely, trying to force the target to commit suicide and condemn their soul to eternity.'"

Bree dropped the page to the floor and sat down awkwardly on the floor against a box. She drew her knees up, bowed her head, tried to get some air.

David stood for a moment, hovering awkwardly, his face shifted in pure terror. But he sat down beside Bree, reached out and rubbed her back, her shoulders.

She leaned against him, crying but tearless. Dry.

She had nothing left.

They sat in the silence for a long moment, listening to the rain beginning to pound down even harder on the roof of the house.

David began to cry softly. Bree, shocked, looked up at him, hot tears beginning to stream down his cheeks. She reached up thoughtfully and wiped them away. His hand caught hers as she did; held it for a moment.

He turned to her, a raging fire in his eyes. A determination that she had never seen before. The next words he said was something she would remember for the rest of her life.

They would haunt her.

"Bree… I don't know what this is that we're truly dealing with here. All I know is that it doesn't appear to be human. At least, not anymore. And it wants to hurt you. Perhaps even kill you.

"But I can promise you this much. With every ounce of strength in my body, with the last breath of my soul… This thing will not win. This thing will not get you. I will protect you. I promise you, Bree. No harm will come to you as long as I'm alive."

His hand gripped hers, tears leaving smears of dirt down his cheeks. Slowly he moved to her, with the rain pelting down dramatically outside, and kissed her softly on the lips.

The kiss, their first, wasn't filled with passion. It was something more simplistic, more basic.

It was pure love. Not a love based around romance, or even one filled with mystique or excitement. It had no bias, no sway. No motivation, no design.

It just was.

She lingered there, tasting him, finally, his lips soft against hers. And then she pulled away, pressing her forehead against his, their hands still entwined.

She burdened a curse.

She didn't have a family.

But she had her Davey.

And for that brief moment on the floor in the blazing light of her grandmother's old living room, that... that was enough.

"I think I found something," David called to her from the attic. He could hear Bree's footfalls on the steps and then she was there, looking suspiciously at the fallen shadows of the attic.

He had turned on as many lights as he could but they still didn't push past the intensity sable darkness that seemed to converge from the corners.

He held out his hand to her and that seemed to appease her.

She went to him, hunkered down on the floor as he pored through an old box that was falling apart.

He held up an old journal and his eyes flashed. Bree grabbed it from him and started flipping through the pages quickly, eyeing the dates with a certain amount of suspicion.

It was her grandmother's old journal. One she kept when she was in her youth. There was an entry that caught her eye. A few years before her father was due to be born.

The hair on the back of her neck stood on end as she read it. Seeming to confirm the madness that emerged from her mother's mouth earlier that day.

Grandma Doris was pregnant once before. The baby given up for adoption for reasons unknown. No known name or address of the child and the people that adopted him. But Bree knew. Somehow she knew...

"Something else," David said as he continued to dig through the box. He pulled out a bundle of old yellowed letters, still in their envelopes, bound with a ribbon.

Bree looked at the address and her blood ran cold.

They were all from Randall Carlisle.

Fingers shaking, Bree pulled a letter free from the stack and pulled the old sheet from the envelope.

"What's it say?" David asked, his eyes already knowing.

She didn't even need to say anything to confirm what they both already knew.

"In short, it claims our suspicions. Grandma Doris' first little baby boy was Randall Carlisle. Carlisle was my uncle."

The room spun around her in a whir. She sat down awkwardly on the floor, once again trying to catch her breath.

Always trying to catch her breath, she thought to herself.

"So that would mean that my father's murder... it wasn't random, Davey. Randall crept into my house that night to kill my father. Because he thought that would break whatever curse was placed on my family? Is that the reason?" Her head shook in the dark.

David replied, "I mean, that's a better motivation than the one that you had before. Which was nothing."

Bree turned to him. "But I saw his eyes that night, Davey. I saw Randall's eyes. They were...wrong. They were black. He... wasn't himself."

David chewed his lip nervously for a moment. Then his eyes shot up to Bree, wild with an idea.

"Bree, you said that Carlisle hanged himself in his cell."

"Yeah. So?"

David reached behind him in the dark and pulled something out of his back pocket. It was the dybbuk printout, folded up and stuffed away. He opened it back up again quickly.

"A dybbuk's entire purpose is to torment its host until they're driven to suicide, damning their soul for eternity. Isn't that right?"

Bree's mouth dropped open.

"Randall... he was... affected too?"

David's head bobbed slightly in the dark.

"You said it was a familial curse, right? Whoever this Francesco is, well, he pissed this spirit off really well."

All of the tumblers slowly started to click into place in Bree's mind. The reporters, the insane media frenzy that drove her to Peru... it wasn't her fault. She didn't say something to Randall that made him kill himself. He was doomed already.

...the media frenzy that led her to Peru...

Suddenly her blood ran cold again. Shivering, she wrapped her arms around herself in the dimly lit attic.

"Davey... where could I have gotten the idea to go to Peru?"

He glanced up at her, not following. "What do you mean?"

"That night, that strange night at your apartment... do you remember you suggested I disappear somewhere for a few weeks. And I instinctively thought of Peru. Why, do you think?"

His brow furrowed in thought for a moment, trying to follow where this was going. "I don't know. Maybe you saw a flier or a pamphlet or something at a newsstand that stuck in your mind. I don't know."

Bree shook her head in the dark.

"No. No, that's not it."

He moved closer to her, waiting patiently to hear what she was about to say.

"Have you ever been asked a question before... I don't know, at work or with your family... they ask you a question and for no real reason at all, you just inherently know the answer? And then you later find out that you were right all along? That's what it felt like when you asked me where I wanted to go. Where I should go. All I could think about was Peru."

David measured her carefully, her face, her tone. There was something shrewdly disturbing about this entire conversation. "Where are you going with this, Bree? You think you were supposed to go down there for some reason?"

"What if... what if the Ouija board was just a small part of it? What if I unleashed this thing with that idiotic moment in time... but what if, what if I needed something to make it more powerful. An object. A talisman of some kind. Like the dybbuk stuff said."

Her fingers fished around in her pocket absentmindedly, finding the beads of the rosary in the dark.

She pulled it out of her pocket, gazed at the name emblazoned now very glaringly on the back of the crucifix. For a moment she couldn't understand why she never saw it before. Until she was meant to.

And that strange stone. The one milky white stone...

Prickles. That familiar feeling she was growing so accustomed to now tickled its way across her body, her blood chilling as she stared more intensely at the rosary.

The white stone, the mysterious milky white stone with black shrouded cloud within...

It was exactly nine stones away from the crucifix.

The ninth stone.

The ninth stone.

"I'm terribly sorry, but office hours are over," a man in creased dress pants and a button-down shirt said to them. They made no move to leave the office. David shut the door behind him softly, the name "Professor Hurley" emblazoned on it.

"Professor Hurley? I'm Breanna Ward." She began, slightly bemused that she was using her real last name again all of a sudden. It just felt right.

Mildly annoyed, he reached out to shake her hand.

"It's a pleasure to meet…" The color drained from his face. He recognized the name, she thought.

"Breanna Ward? Daughter of…"

"Yes. Daughter of Joseph Ward. The man that Carlisle murdered. The very same." She said matter-of-factly. Coolly.

Professor Hurley looked shocked, glancing over at David as if awaiting an explanation. David stood mute, his arms crossed in front of him.

Hurley cleared his throat. "I'm really sorry, but as I've said before, office hours are…"

"We're here on a matter of life and death," Bree began. "I'm sure you're aware of my backstory already, and Randall's involvement in it. Everyone in New York seems to be. But what I need from you is information. Not about Carlisle so much as… as what he was working on when he was arrested."

His eyes narrowed suspiciously. "I'm sorry, I'm confused. I don't understand. Why would you care about what he was working on? He was a professor of archaeology, much the same as me. I'm not sure I understand how the study of a few old dig sites can be a matter of life and death."

Bree shook her head in incredulity.

"I don't have time to explain everything. I just have to ask that you trust me. Trust us."

Again, Hurley glanced over at David, who was giving off an untrustworthy vibe. He was dour, upset, angry. David had a shitty day.

But Bree had honest eyes. Scared eyes.

Hurley relented. He leaned against the back of his desk, running a hand through what was left of his graying hair.

"It was so long ago," he began.

"Please...just remember what you can."

Hurley sighed. "I remember that was right around the time that we were studying the Byzantine Empire in Rome and the eastern Meditterranean. But then..." He stopped. Eyed David again.

"Then what?" Bree urged.

"Then he got... oddly fascinated with South America. Specifically the Inquisitions."

Bree's mouth fell open, nothing coming out. She waited for him to continue. He looked downward to the floor, not seeing her reaction. His mind looked like it was momentarily in a space of time twenty years ago, remembering his friend.

"It was the strangest thing. He was always passionate about history. That part was not unusual. But something lit a fire inside of him. And he was in the office for hours upon end, burning the midnight oil, scouring over old texts and manuscripts, digging deep into the annals of the Peruvian Inquisition."

A chill passed through the room. David noticed and gave her a look. She turned away from him, her eyes focused on Hurley.

"There was a man he was especially inquisitive to find information on. I can't remember his name off-hand…"

"Alter?" David blurted out, wanting to see his reaction.

"Hmm? No, no, not that name. I would have remembered that. No, it was something else…"

Bree cleared her throat. "Francesco?"

Hurley's face shot up, light in his eyes. He snapped his fingers and pointed at her. "Yes! That's it! Francesco! This Francesco guy, he was obsessed over. I'm not sure why, but he did find some information about him."

Bree stood up straight. "Oh? Do you happen to remember what it was that he discovered?"

Hurley groaned. "I mean, it was twenty years ago. A long time. My mind has long been bogged down by other things."

Disappointed, Bree sighed.

"Oh! But I do have his research notes still, I think," he said, moving around to the side of his desk.

"The administration decided to give it to me since we were both professors in the same department after he…" He glanced up briefly towards Bree. "I was sorry to hear about your father."

She smiled wanly. "Thank you. I appreciate it."

He returned her smile and pulled out some keys, unlocking a

drawer and digging through it for a few moments.

"Ah, yes! Here it is." He said, pulling out a large manila file folder with the name "Carlisle" written on the side in black felt ink.

He started to hand it to Bree, and she ripped it open without hesitation. There were a lot of badly written notes, chicken scratch that she couldn't read, a lot of it incredibly unintelligible.

But then there was something her eyes caught hold of immediately. It was typed on a typewriter.

"Davey, listen to this," she said. "It says here that Francesco was born in 1578 in Lima. During his adult years, he was an Inquisitor for the Crown." She looked up at him, terrified.

"What does that mean, Bree?" David asked her, moving over to her.

Her breath came in shallow rasps as her mind tried to wrap itself around what she was reading. "Carlisle had it figured out, Davey. He knew exactly how it all began. It's all right here."

"What is?"

"My fate."

Bree drove through the streets, darkening now with twilight. She ripped through the blocks, not caring or obeying the lights or signs. She had a mission.

"Bree, can you slow down please?" David asked, his hands clinging to the handle on the roof. "You're going too fast in this rain."

"I need to get there, Davey. I need to get there."

"Get where? You still haven't told me what this is all about. What was in those files?"

She turned to him for a moment, her face as white as a ghost. All the blood looked like it had been drained from her. And he noticed dark circles under her eyes.

How long had they been awake? Had they slept? What day was it?

"Bree, what the fuck was in those files?"

"Something, Davey, something that I can't even fathom. But it all makes sense. If you believe. If you believe, it all makes sense."

"You're not making any sense, B. Come on, please slow down!" He cried as they narrowly missed ramming into the side of a pickup truck.

"I'm sorry. I know this is madness right now. But for the first time in my life, Davey. For the first time, I'm seeing things clearly. Francesco, my ancestor. He was a real pile of shit. Power hungry, superiority complex, sadist. Not the best combination of human traits. Randall did his research. That much I give him credit for."

"What happened, B? What happened in Peru?"

Bree drove in silence for a moment, just shaking her head quietly. "The Church. You've heard that the Crown was trying to convert everyone to Catholicism. You've heard of the Spanish Inquisition. They even had one in Mexico. But not many people know about Peru. It lasted hundreds of years. Religious persecution.

I finally know who this Alter was."

"Alter?" The very mention of his name was enough to send chills down David's spine. Bree seemed unfazed.

"Alter was a Jewish monk. He was sent to Peru under the Alhambra Decree in Spain. Just for being a Jew."

David shook his head. "Okay. You're going to have to pretend that I'm not a history major and explain this to me like I'm a child."

Bree sighed, exasperated. "The Alhambra Decree was an edict that the Spanish monarchs issued in the late 1400s. Basically, it stated that all practicing Jews were to be shipped to other territories, one of them being Peru. They were fearful that Jews in the area would convert people away from Catholicism. Those that refused to go would be murdered. Alter was one of the lucky few who was shipped overseas."

David nodded, silent, waiting for more.

"When the Peruvian Inquisition began, it was more of the same. Inquisitors at the time demanded that Jews or Muslims or even recent converts to Catholicism proclaim their faith. If they were fearful to even a small degree that someone was even remotely unaltering in their faith, they were tortured for heresy. It was a scary time for everyone. And guess who Francesco, my ancestor dear, decided to pick on?"

David shook his head, disbelieving. "No way."

"Yes way. Alter himself. Carlisle claims that as Alter was writhing on the pyre, his body in flames, falling off of him in melted chunks, that he was screaming to Francesco that his family and all his offspring would be cursed. Forever tormented by his ghost. That his lineage would be wiped out."

David digested the story for a moment. "Wow. But, but the rosary…"

Bree shook her head in dismay and disgust. "Inquisitors often buried religious artifacts with the bones of the persecuted. Maybe as a final affront to their religion of choice. So of course Alter was buried with a rosary, to mock him for years to come."

David shivered. "That's…that's kind of fucked up." He finally said.

Bree laughed sardonically. "Yes. Yes, it is. No wonder he's so pissed off."

"So where are we rushing off to then?"

Bree sighed. Glanced at him quickly and then averted her eyes.

"The only place I could think to go for help."

She pulled the Jeep in front of a large church and shifted it into Park.

CHAPTER EIGHT
THE DEVIL'S RISING

He leaned forward conspiratorially. Bree did as well, sensing something important was about to be said. Father Thomas glanced over his shoulder sharply, hearing footsteps approach and then eventually diminish. They were alone. David stayed out in the Jeep, giving her privacy.

He looked into Bree's eyes and began in a hushed whisper.

"I am a man of the cloth. I received my calling at a very young age. I studied with the most accomplished theologians in the world. Perhaps that's what led you here today." He started and waited for a response from her.

She sat in silence and nodded slowly, anxious for him to continue.

Father Thomas lowered his head and took off his glasses. He rubbed the bridge of his nose for a moment and sighed deeply. When he looked back up at her, Bree was shocked to see tears brimming his eyes.

"You don't believe. I know. And that's okay. We're meant to question these things, weigh them for ourselves. Faith is ultimately the most important decision you can make. And to believe or disbelieve, it IS a decision."

He looked over her shoulder briefly. A troubled shadow passed over his features.

"Bree," he said, his freckled, plump hand fluttered over hers for a brief moment and then was gone. "You are under attack."

Her blood chilled; the temperature in the room seemed to shift almost imperceptibly. The air became thick and fuzzy; tense. Strange.

She shook her head. "I'm sorry. I'm what?"

"We are often visited by people who need advice, guidance, understanding. They are often afflicted by very tangible things. They come to us because we have the answers. We know the way. We can see the pat. But there are paths that are often so obscured that we do not understand them. We are lights leading the way for our Lord. But there are some shadows that even our lights cannot diminish…"

"What are you saying, Father?"

"Sus ad mortem."

Bree shook her head. "What does that mean?"

Father Thomas took a deep breath. *"Death to the pig."*

Bree's eyes narrowed into slivers, growing frustrated. "Where the hell did you hear that?"

His eyes drifted over her shoulder yet again, his color draining.

"From the man standing behind you."

Bree shifted slightly in her seat, her eyes turning behind her. She couldn't see him but a cold ripple of fear passed through her just the same.

"You mean, you can see him, Father?"

Father Thomas swallowed hard, his eyes still hovering behind her. "Yes."

An urgency rang through Bree's heart. It was getting worse.

"Father, have you ever heard of a dybbuk?"

With that, his eyes finally snapped free of her captor and turned back to her, questioning.

"I have heard of a dybbuk, yes. But I don't hear of them that frequently. Is this what you think you have?" He asked her, no question of whether he believed her.

It was nice to Bree. To be believed automatically.

"Yes. I came here to ask you if you know how to get rid of it. If you know of anyone who ever has."

Father Thomas rubbed the bridge of his nose inquisitively once more and stood up. Started to pace the floor, his eyes deep in thought.

"From what I can recall, a dybbuk is a malicious spirit that clings and infects a host. It usually has a sole purpose, a mission, if you will. And usually they will not relent until that mission has been fulfilled. I've heard of stories where some people have to accomplish some small task in order for the spirit to be satisfied. But that's not always the case." He said, looking over at her, alarmed.

He came back to the pew in front of her and sat down.

"And quite frankly, young lady, based on what I just heard that thing say to me, I think I know exactly what it wants." His hand found hers finally, no longer hovering but thick and weighty on hers. "I'm very sorry."

He got up to leave.

"Wait! What do you mean, 'you're very sorry?' Aren't you going to help me? Please!"

"I'm sorry, Bree. But I cannot help you. The dybbuk will not leave you alone until it gets what it wants. And it appears to want you."

She began to cry. Pulled the rosary from her pocket. Moved over to a candle.

"I'm just going to burn this! Be done with it! Destroy it so that it'll go away and leave me alone!"

Father Thomas moved quickly across the sanctuary and caught her wrist in the air.

"Now listen to what I'm telling you. This is very important. You must not burn the talisman. It seems a logical thing to do, to destroy whatever fostered this being into this world, but trust me when I tell you it is a grave mistake. You will be unleashing the dybbuk into the world forever. You would be granting it exactly what it wants: unlimited power and strength. Without this intact for it to return to, it will be left to roam the earth. Do not, I repeat, do *not* destroy this!"

Bree crumpled to a pew, grasping the cursed rosary in her hands. She looked up at Father Thomas, tears streaking down her face.

"What more can I do, Father?" She asked, her voice already despairing.

Father Thomas met her gaze, his own eyes welling with tears, and whispered, "Pray."

He walked away, his footsteps receding like empty echoes down the corridor. Bree glanced up at the giant crucifix of Christ and suddenly grew very angry. Her fists closed around the rosary, the edges of the crucifix biting into her flesh, warm blood flowing angrily down her palm.

She would do anything else. But she refused to pray. It was all of that religious garbage that got her into this mess in the first place.

Fuming, she stood up from the pew and walked outside.

"What did he say?" David asked eagerly when she finally crawled back into the Jeep. She was morose for a moment, quiet. Bree put the rosary back into the depths of her jacket pocket.

"He said to go home."

She started the Jeep and began the long drive back to the city.

The stairwell was dark when she walked through the doorway. Bree shifted the paper grocery bag uncomfortably on her hip as she shut the door with her foot.

Groaning, she began her ascent in the dark, making a mental note to call Breyden in the morning to complain. First the elevators, now the lights. God forbid one of his tenants should fall down the staircase and hurt themselves.

It had been a long day at Riley & Wendt. Deposition after deposition; a neverending stream of domestic abuse cases, homicides, manslaughters, child custody, divorce. The world was going to hell in a handbasket, Bree thought to herself with a smug smile.

She'd be the first in line.

Her bosses had been very generous with her time off, considering what she had recently been through. They were also thankful they didn't have a public relations circus on their hands. Her boss practically pushed her out the door to go on her vacation.

Peru seemed like a distant memory now. It had only been a few weeks since she returned but a demanding job with twelve-hour days was again beginning to take its toll. She knew that she had be patient. That eventually all of her hard work and the long hours would pay off.

A few flights up, she stopped to catch her breath.

A door somewhere in the stairwell latched shut. It echoed through the dark down to her.

The building was six stories high in the middle of SoHo. Her apartment wasn't large and she was struggling to pay rent, but it was rent-controlled and she had no intention of moving. She hadn't met many of her neighbors, as work demanded the majority of her time. The only time she spent at her apartment was on the weekends, staring mindlessly at the television decompressing from the previous week.

Only to get up early on Monday morning and continue the entire charade all over again.

She heard footsteps coming down the stairs and anticipated putting a smile on her tired face and saying hello to one of her fellow stranger/neighbors.

But the footsteps stopped just as the person should have rounded the bend. Bree waited a moment, and then called out, "Hello?"

She heard her voice echo throughout the stairwell and fall flat.

No answer.

Shrugging, she continued up the next flight of stairs and turned.

No one was there.

Old buildings were funny places, she told herself. She often heard things, shifts and creaks, and was growing rather accustomed to them. But she was pretty certain she had heard footsteps.

She groaned as she glanced up and realized she still had another four flights to go. Bree grumbled to herself quietly, cursing Breyden for being so cheap.

She was reaching the 5th floor landing when she heard it.

At first it sounded like the mere hissing of wind coming through the stairwell air duct. But instead of maintaining a consistent tone, it began to crescendo.

The hairs on Bree's arm began to rise.

There was something in the stairwell with her.

She knew it immediately, instinctively. There was a change in the air, a de minimis shift. It became hard to breathe. The air felt almost static, electric.

"BBBBRRRRRRREEEEEEEEEEEEEEEEEEEEEEE......" The sound began to change, forming a word.

Her name.

She glanced over the rail into the dark stairwell below her, her heart thudding loudly in her chest. At first she saw nothing. The building was abnormally quiet for an evening hour. All of her neighbors' doors were shut tightly and locked.

Under the eave of the 4th flight, she saw a movement in the shadows. A gnarled hand, hidden mostly under the sleeve of a heavy, brown cloak, gripped the railing.

Bree slowly backed away, but she could not divert her eyes from the figure that was gradually emerging from under the eave to glance upward towards her.

From out of the shadows it came, only to be momentarily awashed by the meager moonlight streaming in through the dinghy skylight high above. A hooded head came out into the moonlight and began to turn upward towards her.

She first saw his smile. Wide. Abnormally wide. His teeth were ancient, knobby and jutting out in awkward directions. But they were sharp. Bree could see that in the dark.

Very sharp.

Saliva dripped from his mouth, coating his hand and the railing in a slippery dew. And then his eyes rose to meet hers.

Bree gasped. Her eyes widened and she dropped the bag of groceries.

"BRRRREEEEEEE….." His horrid mouth opened and her name emitted into the stairwell, echoing up to her quickly. He began to move. He moved quickly up the stairs, surprisingly agile for however ancient an abomination he was.

Bree burst into a run, hearing him tripping over the rolling cans of Spaghetti O's and refried beans that littered the staircase behind her.

How did he catch up to her so quickly? Bree thought madly as she sprinted up the stairs. She could hear her own rapid breathing, forced and difficult. Beyond that, nothing. The man wasn't even breaking a sweat.

"BRRRRREEEEEEE…." He called out to her again, and she

burst into tears.

His voice was suddenly different.

It wasn't.

It couldn't be.

Her heart felt like it was going to stop; her lungs felt like they were going to burst. It became difficult to see through her tears.

Any moment she waited to feel his gnarled grip on her shoulder, to pull her back and over the railing, to flail to her death below. But it didn't come.

She sensed he was right behind her.

The call came again.

"BRRRREEEE....."

He was directly behind her. But it was a woman's voice now.

If she wasn't so terrified, her instinct likely would have been to stop and face the creature. The voice was familiar.

Loving.

Haunting.

"No! It can't be!" She sobbed into the dark stairwell and rounded the bend to the last flight. Bree could see her apartment door; the letters 6A never seemed so inviting.

She shoved her hands into the pocket of her jeans as she bolted up the last set of stairs, fishing out her key. Her legs felt like they were going to buckle underneath her. She screamed loudly into the stairwell, hoping the sound would drive her neighbors out to help.

...just in case she couldn't get her door open in time...

She finally reached her door and fumbled with her key, suddenly forgetting which one it was.   Her eyes were foggy with tears and mascara; it was hard to see in the dark.

Fuck Breyden.

But she didn't dare look back.

She couldn't look back.

She waited for the fingers. For the hand to grip her shoulder.

Finally the key slid easily into the hole and she twisted, opened the door, flew inside.

Just as she shut the door, she caught another glimpse. The figure slowly stalked up the stairs, eyeing her.   That broad, demented, diabolical smile never faltering.

She shut the door and immediately bolted it. Chained.

Grabbed her heavy oak console table and pushed it against the door, knocking her lamp and telephone off its ringer in the meantime.

Bree flew over to her small living room, dove onto the floor and reached under the sofa. She felt the cool metal and sighed softly.

She always kept it loaded. Bree flicked the safety off and waited. Watching the door.

She had little hope that this would help her at all against what was waiting outside her door.

Bree hunkered down behind her coffee table, her arms shaky and wavering yet steadily aiming her 9mm towards the quiet door. Her mind began to process everything that had occurred in the last few minutes.

She had seen this man many times before; knew his name. And that voice… it turned into…

Bree shook her head, trying to clear the insane thought. It couldn't be.

"Okay, Bree, get it together. Get it together," she said to herself softly, her cheeks still damp with tears, her forehead clammy with sweat. Try as she might, she couldn't stop shaking. Her heart, she feared, might never beat normally again.

She wasn't sure exactly what she was trying to get together, or even how to reconcile what she had experienced, because it was beyond the scope of normal.

It was impossible.

What had just happened was impossible…

But then everything else up to that point had seemed impossible. The most frightening thing about this situation, however, was that it was very real. Very violent. And it was definitely getting worse…

Suddenly the door to her apartment exploded, pieces of wood flying through the air.

She screamed, closed her eyes, and squeezed four shots out towards the entrance.

"Shit!! Oh God, no…." She begged.

When she opened her eyes, there was no one there.

The obliterated apartment door lied scattered around her apartment in pieces. Beyond the threshold, the dark, black corridor.

He was gone.

She sat there the rest of the night, her gun aimed towards the open maw of what used to be her apartment door, crying and growing even more sure of one thing.

Alter wasn't going to stop hunting her until she was dead.

"I'm really sorry, Davey. I didn't know who else to call," she stuttered, throwing her overnight bag on his sofa. She had grabbed a handful of clothes and all of the pills in her medicine cabinet and ran from her apartment.

"Oh Jesus, Bree. You don't need to apologize. You should know better than that by now."

"Do you... do you have some wine or something? Maybe something a little harder?" Bree asked him, sitting down on the sofa, her hands shaking.

"Of course," he replied, returning from the kitchen a moment later with a couple of glasses filled with ice and a bottle of vodka. He poured them both a quick drink and handed it to her.

She sipped it gratefully, her eyes watching him over the brim. Her eyes were bloodshot with dark circles underneath. The skin on her face seemed pallid and her cheekbones protruded more than he noticed before.

He threw his drink back in one long swallow. She took a couple sips of hers and nursed it for a moment.

"I don't know what to think about all of this," she began.

David nodded in agreement. There wasn't much left to say between the two of them.

"I'm just so tired, Davey." Her voice wavered, but tears didn't come. "I'm just so goddamned tired. Of it all. Of this life."

He moved over to sit next to her on the sofa, wrapping his arm around her, pulling her close. He could tell that she wanted to cry, let it all out, but she didn't. She held back. Held it in.

She turned her face up to his, her lips dry and cracked and almost bleeding.

In her soft voice, she murmured, "I'm scared."

David nodded slowly and pulled her head against his chest again, running his fingers through her hair.

"I am, too."

They sat that way for a long while, in a stretched, comfortable silence. Imperceptibly something had changed. It was as if a dark shadow had passed over their heads and it was not going away.

Something sinister was coming. Of that they were certain.

But for right now, that very moment, they had each other.

Though they were quite certain it wouldn't be for long…

Bree was asleep in the bed, the soft moonlight falling across her cheek when David was cleaning up the kitchen. He threw the vodka glasses into the sink, looked guiltily at the empty bottle and tossed it in the trash.

It was a rough day.

A rough week.

A rough life.

He moved through the small apartment, clicking off lights as he went. As he moved down the corridor, he tripped on Bree's overnight bag.

Caught himself quickly before he fell. A few items had scattered to the floor so he kneeled down to put them back in the bag.

That's when he saw it.

The rosary.

Lying on the floor, harmless, innocuous, benign.

But David knew better.

Angry, he picked it up and held it up in the moonlight. The crucifix swayed around innocently, twisting and twirling in his hand, until it turned backwards and he saw the name "Alter" engraved on the back, taunting him.

It was that moment.

A well of anger and frustration and worry and concern over Bree just brewed inside of him like a spring. Suddenly, tears sprang to his eyes and he became furious.

"You fucker. You want to come into my house and mess with my girl and her family? You've got another thing coming," he spoke out loud to the dangling rosary.

He imagined he looked ridiculous, speaking so angrily at an inanimate object, but he didn't care. David was through.

Done.

It was time to show this Alter who was boss.

He bent over to the nearby coffee table, picked up the small gas insert fireplace remote control and hit a button.

In a flash, a fire erupted from the fireplace, burning warmly in just a few moments. He could hear Bree's heavy breathing in the other room, passed out from sheer exhaustion.

He'd take care of this, and Bree would be free in the morning.

No more Alter.

No more dybbuk.

No more ghosts.

Just him and Bree and a lifetime for him to try to make her happy.

He opened the hinged door eagerly, and held the dangling object up just one more time in front of his face.

"Rot in hell," he murmured one last time and threw the rosary on the dancing flames.

It lay there on the embers for just a moment, and then there was a pop of life from the dancing flames. The fire grew hotter for a moment, much brighter than before. And then the rosary was alight.

Blackening, curling, melting all over the heating unit in the fireplace. He didn't care about the mess.

He smiled as he watched it char and burn.

After a long moment, and he was satisfied that it was completely destroyed, he clicked a button and the fireplace went dark.

He turned off the last lamp in the living room and went to bed.

CHAPTER NINE
THE POSSESSION

That night, they slept side by side in his bed, Bree's head resting in the crook of his arm.

He felt her move against him in the dark, her hand suddenly reaching out and running the length of his chest.

She was pressed up against him in the darkness before he was able to open his eyes and realize what was happening.

"David," she whispered to him, her voice subtle and seductive. And a little strange. The sound of her voice, husky and delicate, made his body respond before he could even help himself.

Her hand wandered to the nape of his neck, ran up his jawline; her fingers (had they always been this dry?) caressing his ear lobe as she moved in closer, her mouth hovering inches from his.

It wasn't until her lips were on his, chapped and cold and stiff and strange, that he realized what she had just called him.

David.

Bree never called him David. For as long as he'd known her, it was always Davey.

Something was wrong.

He began to pull away from the kiss but Bree moved against him roughly, refusing to give him any room to escape. Her cold hands gripped the back of his head, refusing to give him any space to move.

"Bree, what…" He tried to say, but Bree's teeth clamped down hard on his bottom lip, grinding and drawing blood until David began to scream. With a savage loud rip, he felt a strange tug and then suddenly the kiss came free. It made a sickening suction sound, one that made him nauseas to hear, and then a white, hot pain ripped through his mouth. He realized what had just happened.

She ripped off his lip with her teeth.

All of a sudden, she was on top of him, straddling him, naked and awash in the moonlight. The curves of her body in the dim light was something he had always fantasized about, dreamed about. But not like this.

He thrashed around, trying to break free from underneath Bree. But Bree was suddenly very heavy, very solid, and immovable. He knew it was futile.

He knew this was not Bree.

Despite his best efforts, he felt his body responding. Sobs ripped from his throat as blood seeped into his mouth from the gaping wound where his lip had been. She felt him harden against her and she began to writhe on top of him, teasing him.

"Oh, you like it rough? You have no idea what you're in for," she taunted, teased, no longer Bree's voice but something different. Someone different.

He tried to call out but he was choking on his own blood. David was struggling to get air, let alone enough to scream. He wanted to beg, he wanted to plead, he wanted to fight. But he knew it would be futile.

All he could do was pray. Pray for it to be over soon. Pray for everything to end.

Despite his deepest hopes, he sputtered out a bloody, "Bree…"

She only laughed, a deep, maniacal laugh that seemed to echo off the walls of the apartment bedroom walls.

"You're smarter than that by now, aren't you? Catch up, *Davey*," she said the last part taunting, teasing.

He felt the creature move against him once more and suddenly, he was inside of it. It moved on top of him sensually, swaying its hips in the moonlight seductively. It looked a little like Bree, but it was changing. It's skin was turning almost a decayed looking hue. Almost blue in the moonlight. Dry. Very dry. Flaking off. Falling apart. Each thrust brought David an immense searing pain through his groin. It was as if this thing had a bag full of glass, sharp and tearing and eating him alive.

"I thought this is what you wanted. You always wanted her. So now you have her," the thing hissed at him as it thrust again and again, harder and harder.

There was no pleasure to be had with this creature on top of him. That was slowly morphing and changing into something that he couldn't even begin to describe. It was so dry, like sandpaper, against him, rubbing and chafing and scraping and biting and clawing…

He began to feel blood, warm and thick, coursing down the length of him. As she thrust over him, he could see her breasts were beginning to change from the supple shapely mounds that he had always dreamed of kissing, to sagging, haggard deflated bags of rotting flesh. Her hair, once full and thick, was now coarse and thin, hanging in strings down her back.

And her face. Her mouth, those lips he had kissed so gently, were gone. Now only drenched in blood, thin and drawn in, the teeth around them sharp and pointed.

Hungry.

She rode him harder, every thrust scraping and biting and tearing and clawing at him. He tried to cry out in pain, for it all to stop, but was met with only the gurgling of blood from his torn mouth. Every time he tried, the creature laughed and rode him harder. He felt like every bit of himself was shredded flesh, pulpy and bloody and non-recognizable.

The thing reached out and grabbed his wrists, held them above his head as it leaned its face in closer to his.

"You shouldn't have fucking burned the rosary." It hissed, taunting, and then thrust once more, very hard, and David tried to scream but couldn't. Something strange had just happened; he felt lighter, adrift, less than.

It wasn't until he looked up into the things merciless black eyes that he realized what happened.

It was gone.

That piece of him was gone. He could feel the blood gushing and pooling between his thighs.

His eyes fluttered and he passed out.

David drifted in and out of unconsciousness. When he came to, pain inflamed every inch of his body. He glanced over to the side of the bed and didn't see the creature.

No longer Bree.

Bree was gone.

Bree was no more.

He knew this.

Instinctively.

Like a bird knows how to fly when it's young.

Like a child knows how to nurse on its mother.

He just knew.

His Bree.

Suddenly, images of her smile, the sound of her laugh, the scent of her hair, the flash in her eyes when she really found something funny.

His Bree was no more.

And that knowledge hurt him more than anything else.

More than anything that was bitten or ripped or torn off of his body.

He wanted to die. He just lay there in his bedroom, blood smeared all over his face, his chest, his bedsheets, and willed himself to die. He couldn't bring himself to look lower, to see what had been done to his body when he was passed out. If the pain was any indicator, though, he didn't doubt that he was missing other vital appendages.

He coughed and spit up blood.

He tried to cry.

He couldn't cry.

His body was dried.

Hollowed out.

Done.

This indignity.

This death.

And he couldn't even muster a final cry.

One last sob.

As the blood rushed from his body, seeping into the worn blue carpet of his bedroom, he thought of Bree.

He thought of Bree.

He thought of Bree…

"All your fault! It's all your fault!"

Her mother's voice screamed out at her. Hollow and strange. Echoing.

Reverberating through her head.

It felt odd, like one of those strobe lights that was always a second or two lagged. Always trying to catch up.

She could see the things in front of her. She could see the soft moonlight streaming in through the window of David's room. But she couldn't turn her head. Couldn't move her hand.

A ripple of terror struck her.

Something was very, very wrong.

And then the awful.

The hideous.

The absolutely terrible things that she could see herself doing to poor David.

Powerless to stop herself.

Powerless to stop the fiend.

She knew that she was losing. Losing the delicate battle she had been fighting for so long.

David lie still on the bed, covered in blood and gore. She could taste his blood on her lips, metallic and fresh. He was soaked in crimson. Unrecognizable.

Bree wanted to cry. Wanted to sob. Hold him. Cradle his head. Kiss him. Do all the things she felt every urge in her soul to do.

But her body wouldn't allow it.

He was gone. She was sure of it.

And what little will she had left, what little fight she had left in her, was gone.

It was a thought.

Just a sliver of a second of a thought.

Only a momentary inclination of defeat. To have this thing, whatever it was, do its bidding already, to be done with what it had to do...

And she lost.

Relinquished control.

She could see herself getting up from the bloody bed. Walk over to her overnight bag.

All of the pills she had stored in her medicine cabinet, every single bottle of Prozac and Celexa and Paxil and Norpramin and Pamelor;

she grabbed everything.

At the time she wasn't sure why. It wasn't like she was taking any of these on a semi-regular basis.

But now she knew. His design.

His plan.

What he wanted.

And she willed it to be done.

There was no more Davey. No one else. Nothing else to live for.

The dybbuk had done its job.

Like Hamlet, she admitted her fate.

…there is special providence in the fall of a sparrow…

…"What does it matter what I believe?"…

…"I think you'll find that it will, Bree."…

It had sucked her dry of any desire to live, to fight.

It had robbed her of everything good and pure in her life.

What little of it she had left.

David. Her stalwart supporter. The man who stood beside her through some impossibly stressful situations.

Things that no human should ever have to endure, he felt it with her.

For her.

Unbending.

Immovable.

Dead.

She grabbed the pills and went into the bathroom.

Began to draw a bath.

Looked in the mirror.

And was shocked at what she saw.

There was someone standing in front of the mirror.

But it wasn't her.

The lips, small and narrow, were covered and drenched in blood. The teeth protruding over the lips were sharp and dripping with bile. The face itself was gaunt, hollowed out, the flesh snapping across the top in tight, dry ribbons. Scaly, almost. The eyes…

…oh sweet God, the eyes…

…were an unending black. No iris, no hue. Just pure black.

She had seen those eyes before…

She turned to the bath, the water almost scalding hot. Without another thought, she put one leg into the hot water, bubbling and gurgling around her scaly flesh. Blistering and peeling.

The other leg then, and finally she sank down into the rising water, the faucet running tirelessly.

Popped open the first bottle. She didn't see or even care what it was she took first.

Tossed the entire bottle of pills into her mouth at once. Ran a scaly hand into the water, gobbled it up thirstily, washing down the pills.

Then another bottle.

Then another.

Another.

A few minutes later and things began to get hazy. Like an old vignette on a photo, the edges turning black.

Narrow.

She waited.

Just a little while longer.

Suddenly, there was a ripping feeling of extreme pain. The scalding water was blistering her flesh and she felt every second of it. She looked up.

She was queasy, fading in and out, the pain around her, inside her, encapsulating her very existence.

And in her delirium, she looked up.

She was face to face with Alter.

He stared at her, a strange grin playing around his mouth.

Her eyes bobbed, heavy, somnambulant. She wanted to sleep.

"I…I'm sorry," she whispered, unsure if he heard the words.

Alter didn't say anything. He just sat and smiled at her.

Bree's head bobbed again, very close to the water this time, threatening to drown.

Drops of hot water slipped over the edge of the bathtub, the faucet still running on full blast.

"Sorry." Alter mocked, his lips curled in a snarl. "A word. A mere word." He stated snidely. "I, myself. I like words. Another word: revenge. This one is perhaps my favorite."

Bree fell back against the back of the tub. She felt herself fading into blackness, into unconsciousness.

And she thought, all things considered, especially compared to poor Davey, this would be a better way to go.

"Another word: promise." He went on.

"I made a promise a long time ago. And a man is only as good as his word." He leaned closer to Bree, whispering sharply in her ear. "I have one final word for you, Breanna. Do you know what it is?"

The blackness ebbed and flowed around her. The scalding water threatened to drown her if it should take hold.

Her David was dead. Her family was dead.

She had wandered this path, this path to Alter, to this final moment in a small cramped bathroom, in a horrid bathtub, since she was a little girl. Everything was leading up to this moment.

And she knew.

She knew the word.

Her eyelids flickered open, then shut.

Her head slowly began to sink under the depths of the steaming water.

But her lips.

Her lips uttered the word.

"Fate."

THE END

ABOUT THE AUTHOR

Angela Darling is a novelist who lives in the Seattle area. Dubbed "The Queen of the Macabre," her novels are richly infused with history, romance and dark gothic horror. Her biggest writing influences include Edgar Allan Poe, V.C. Andrews and Shirley Jackson.

She has been writing for over 30 years, completing her first full-length novel, "War" when she was just 15 years old.